PRAISE FOR
BAD NEWS TRAVELS FAST

"*Bad News Travels Fast* has the same kind of tight, nervous energy as the Gunner books and much more substance than most so-called "comic" thrillers . . . The plotline of *Bad News Travels Fast* has some interesting and timely twists, but it's Haywood's sharp words in Dottie Loudermilk's mouth that give the book an extra kick, especially for people with adult children."
—*Chicago Tribune*

"Haywood gets the narrating [of] Dottie's voice just right; she meets her grown children with a delightfully entertaining blend of frustration and devotion."
—*Publishers Weekly*

"Weird and wonderful adventures . . . an irresistibly rollicking riposte to the family-values crowd."
—*Kirkus Reviews*

"Like its predecessor, *Going Nowhere Fast, Bad News* is good fun."
—*Detroit News & Free Press*

"Wonderful, well-conceived characters who transcend race. Long-suffering parents and long-married couples everywhere will recognize kindred spirits and enjoy their adventures."
—*Los Angeles Daily News*

continued

"I love this novel so much I want to give copies to everyone I know. From now on, I'm following Joe and Dottie in the great Airstream trailer of life."
—Nancy Pickard

"*Going Nowhere Fast* is going somewhere *real* fast, and the going is pure delight!"
—Karen Kijewski

"A masterful mystery writer . . . Haywood's the real thing. Not everyone can tell a story in the way it should be told. Gar Anthony Haywood is just such a writer and one deserving of greater attention."
—*Chicago Tribune*

"Mothers are the most maligned figures in life and literature. But thanks to Gar Anthony Haywood's new protagonist, women with children have a voice: witty, persevering Dottie Loudermilk, mother of five dysfunctional grown-up kids and the wife of a man in love with his Airstream. Haywood has created a wise and compassionate character. All right, so Mr. Haywood is a man. But God, he knows his women."
—Melodie Johnson Howe

"Terrific . . . the funniest book I've read this year."
—*Detroit Free Press*

Also by Gar Anthony Haywood

GOING NOWHERE FAST
YOU CAN DIE TRYING
NOT LONG FOR THIS WORLD
FEAR OF THE DARK

BAD
NEWS
TRAVELS
FAST

Gar Anthony Haywood

BERKLEY PRIME CRIME, NEW YORK

This Prime Crime Book contains the complete text of the hardcover edition. It has been completely reset in a typeface designed for easy reading and was printed from new film.

BAD NEWS TRAVELS FAST

A Berkley Prime Crime Book / published by arrangement with the author

PRINTING HISTORY
G.P. Putnam's Sons edition published 1995
Berkley Prime Crime edition / September 1996

The Putnam Berkley World Wide Web site address is
http://www.berkley.com

ISBN: 0-425-15464-5

Berkley Prime Crime Books are published
by The Berkley Publishing Group,
200 Madison Avenue, New York, NY 10016.
The name BERKLEY PRIME CRIME and the BERKLEY PRIME CRIME design are trademarks belonging to Berkley Publishing Corporation.

PRINTED IN THE UNITED STATES OF AMERICA

10 9 8 7 6 5 4 3 2 1

ACKNOWLEDGMENTS

Any resemblance the real Washington, D.C., may have to the city depicted in this book can be attributed solely to the following people, to whom the author is eternally grateful:

DEBBIE KNUTSON
Mystery Books

BETH SINIAWSKY
Executive Assistant to the
Honorable Eddie Bernice Johnson

DAVID SCHERTLER
U.S. Attorney's Office

LISA SWAYNE

and the CompuServe Commandos:

JOE LACEY
TOM JONES
GEORGE L. LEVENTHAL

This one's for my little women:

Courtney Marie

and

Erin Elizabeth

Daddy's girls forever

BAD
NEWS
TRAVELS
FAST

Lincoln's eyes moved.

At least, that was what the crazy woman doing all the shouting was insisting. "I saw his eyes move! He looked right at me! I saw his eyes move!" she screamed, moving from tourist to tourist like a hummingbird flitting from chrysanthemum to chrysanthemum, trying to get people to look. Those that humored her were disappointed, of course; the huge stone centerpiece of the Lincoln Memorial remained unfazed, eyes fixed as firmly and implacably on the crystalline pool facing the monument as they had been since its opening in 1922.

The crazy woman's husband, meanwhile, was mortified. They were both too old for this. She was creating an incredible scene, and all eyes (other than Abraham Lincoln's, unfortunately) were on his wife. They had traveled hundreds of miles to visit Washington, D.C., fulfilling one of his lifelong

1

dreams, and this, no doubt, was going to be the highlight of their trip: being fitted for straitjackets on the steps of the Lincoln Memorial on a dark and humid August afternoon.

"I saw his eyes move! Really! They looked right at me!"

She was now yanking on the sleeve of a tall, square-jawed fellow in a Washington Redskins warm-up jacket, trying to pull him closer to the giant statue. He wasn't budging.

Her husband tried to break her grip on the poor man, but couldn't. He was aware now that people had finally connected them as a couple, and were waiting for him to assert some authority and take charge of the situation.

They didn't know his wife very well.

Inevitably, one of the Memorial's security guards came over to try and rein the madwoman in himself, but he only ended up chasing her about like a cowboy trying to rope a calf. The crowd roared. The husband moaned. A second security guard joined in the chase to heighten the hilarity. It all made for a free show no one expected to get, but everyone was overjoyed to receive.

Finally, two uniformed police officers appeared out of nowhere to break things up. They sliced through the crowd expertly and took the hysterical woman into custody with surprisingly little muss or fuss. The mere sight of them seemed to take all the fight out of her.

"Take it easy now, ma'am," one of them said as they put the handcuffs on her. "Everything's going to be okay."

"But I saw his eyes move," she told them, making the claim one last time just for effect.

The two officers just nodded their heads and walked her gingerly down the Memorial's steps to their waiting police car.

Following close behind, the woman's humiliated husband mumbled something quietly under his breath.

"Jeez Looweez," he said.

___ 1 __

But I'm getting ahead of myself.

Stories are meant to be told from the beginning, not from somewhere near the end. And the beginning of this story comes five days before the "Psycho Grandma on Drugs Visits the Lincoln Memorial" episode I've just described.

So let me back up a little.

I went bonkers at the feet of Honest Abe on a Saturday. The previous Monday, my husband Big Joe and I were on the road, headed north on Interstate 95 in Virginia, less than thirty miles south of the nation's capital. We were on the road because that's where the two of us live now, on the road. We're what are known in some circles as "fulltimers": globetrotting trailer home owners with no permanent address.

People become fulltimers for many different reasons, but Joe and I have more reasons than most. Five, to be exact. Their names are Maureen, Delila, Walter, Edward, and

Theodore. These are our children, as you may have already guessed. Grown children by chronological standards, but hardly out of pubescence in terms of emotional maturity. In fact, with the lone exception of Maureen (whom we all refer to as ''Mo''), these characters are the most consistently annoying human beings on this earth. They go to school, but take pains not to learn anything remotely useful; they seek and find employment, only to see who can be shown the door the fastest. They date weird people and adhere to Mickey Mouse religions. They give birth to grandchildren from hell and raise them like pet goldfish won at a church carnival. And they borrow money from their parents the way some European nations borrow from the U.S. government: by the trillions. Only the Defense Department spends money faster.

So when the time came for Joe and me to retire early—he from the El Segundo, California, Police Department, and I from the faculty of Loyola Marymount University—the question wasn't how often we'd like to leave home, but how fast we could get out of town, and where we could best hide for the remainder of our lives. As things turned out, the answer to the first question was, as fast as we could sell our home (three months), and the answer to the second, nowhere and everywhere. Home for Joe and Dottie Loudermilk now is the open highway, and while that has taken some getting used to, it has had the desired effect of making us almost impossible to find when (a) Delila wants to introduce us to her latest psychotic husband; (b) Walter needs investors for his partner's waterless Jacuzzi; (c) Theodore has to sell 150 boxes of Afrocentric Hanukkah cards in mid-June to avoid another lawsuit; or (d) Edward is looking for a place to lay low so as to avoid running into one of his knife-wielding ex-girlfriends.

If you're beginning to feel an ulcer coming on just listening to this, I believe I've made my point.

They're our kids, and we love them, but Joe and I figured we could love them just as well from a distance of several hundred miles as we could from our old living room, and at far less expense. Hence, the ink wasn't dry on our retirement questionnaires when we hit the ground running and told Mo, our newly elected financial manager–slash–family liaison, "Don't call us, we'll call you."

That was almost two years ago.

Since that time, Big Joe and I have put over forty-five thousand miles on our Ford Lightning pickup and twenty-seven-foot Airstream trailer home, hopping from one resort city or state park to the next, with no discernible method to our madness. We go where our collective whim takes us, and we stay as long as we like. It's a great life for two old geezers in their mid-fifties; every day is different, every day brings something new.

And none of our heartbreaking, debt-inducing kids are around to spoil the fun.

Usually.

I mean, we have on a few rare occasions crossed paths with one or two of our children, but not because we ever planned it that way. Perhaps we accidentally ran into the child, or fell victim to some unfortunate breach of security that enabled him or her to track us down like a pair of escaped killers last seen on *America's Most Wanted*. After all the trouble and expense we've gone to to avoid any further contact with our unholy offspring, it would be criminal for one of us to actually arrange a rendezvous with one of them. Absolutely criminal.

Which is why I've only done it once, up to now.

"Did you say Eddie?" Big Joe asked. This was on a Monday, if you recall what I said earlier. Out on Interstate 95, thirty miles shy of Washington, D.C.

"Yes," I said.

"*Our* Eddie?"

"Our son Eddie, yes."

"And you said—"

"That we'll be meeting him for dinner tonight. Yes."

He hadn't taken his eyes off the road yet, and that worried me.

"Says who?" he finally asked, turning. I imagined an egg on the top of his beautifully bald brown head, frying sunny side up with the snap, crackle, and pop of bacon grease.

"Joe, we are not going to argue about this," I said flatly.

"You're darn right we're not."

"Joe—"

"That boy is a lost cause, Dottie. He's over the edge."

"Just because his politics don't agree with ours—"

"You call it politics. I call it psychobabble. Anti-American psychobabble."

"Joe, he is *not* anti-American. He just . . . happens to see America a little differently than most people, that's all."

Joe cocked his head at me and raised an eyebrow, declining to even dignify my statement with a retort. Saying our son Eddie saw America a little differently than most folks was like saying the Beatles once had a somewhat different view of haircuts than most ex-Marines. The truth was, Eddie was an extremist where his politics were concerned, to the extent that he saw a government conspiracy around every corner. If the phone company made a mistake on his bill, it was because the F.B.I. had tapped into the phone company's computer and fouled things up trying to monitor his calls. If his cable company lost its C-SPAN signal for more than six minutes, it was proof that Congress didn't want the average American to know what kind of corrupt business it was cooking up next. Joe liked to say the boy couldn't lick a stamp for fear the U.S. Postal Service was poisoning the glue—and I had to admit, that was only a slight exaggeration.

"All right," I said finally. "So he does have a screw or two loose, I'll grant you that. But that doesn't mean we can't sit down and have a meal with the child, does it?"

"What's he doing in Washington? Did you ask him that?"

"He said he was here with some friends. They've formed some kind of political action committee."

"Uh-huh." Joe was nodding his head at the road ahead, congratulating himself for having predicted I would say something along those lines.

"They're here to lobby against some bill, Joe. Not blow up the Washington Monument."

"That's how they all get started, terrorists. 'Lobbying.' One minute they're passing out leaflets, and the next they're chucking grenades."

"Oh, don't be ridiculous . . ."

"Ridiculous?"

"Yes, ridiculous. The boy may be spacey, but he isn't insane."

"Well, call it what you will. Whatever Eddie's condition is, it makes for lousy dinner conversation, and I'm in no mood to hear it. All right?"

"Joe—"

"I said, forget it. You just call that boy the minute we get to the trailer park and tell him we can't make it. We'll catch him at Mo's this Thanksgiving, or Christmas, or whenever."

When I didn't answer that, he turned again to face me, determined to both see and hear me acquiesce.

"Whatever you say, baby," I said.

Thirty-seven years I've been using that line, and he still thinks it means, "Okay."

Six hours later, I was getting the silent treatment.

Since the realization struck him that we really were going to have dinner with Eddie after all, when he'd found himself naked and in the shower where I'd practically had to carry him, Big Joe hadn't said a word to me. Not one. He thought he was inflicting a punishment, because that's what silence always was whenever I used it on him, but like many men, he didn't understand that a husband holding his tongue is more an aphrodisiac to a woman than a torture. I mean, really, girls, what is it we're supposed to miss hearing when the old man clams up? The latest ball scores?

Oh, the agony.

Anyway, Joe wasn't talking, and I wasn't complaining, when we arrived at the address Eddie had given me, just a few minutes before seven in the evening. It was a lovely little two-story town house in an area called Dupont Circle, north of Capitol Hill proper on the eastern outskirts of Georgetown. This was reportedly one of Washington's most vibrant and colorful neighborhoods, very big with the art crowd, Eddie had said, and it had that look: outdoor cafés were in cheerful abundance and lavishly muraled walls seemed to mark every street corner. We must have passed a dozen lush, green parks just looking for a parking space.

"This is beautiful," I said as we stood on the porch, waiting for someone to answer the bell.

Joe just turned his slitted eyes in my direction and grunted. He was unhappy to be here, primarily, but I knew that there was more to his foul mood than that. Besides being ticked off at me, he was suffering from withdrawal. Big Joe is always on edge immediately after we've left

Lucille—that's Joe's pet name for our trailer, believe it or not, Lucille—behind in some trailer park after having been on the road with her for days. He loves her that much. He's like a seaman on his first day of shore leave: solid earth feels unnatural beneath his feet.

Usually, all you can do is wait for him to get over it.

Which is exactly what I was doing when the door suddenly flew open and Eddie cried, "Mom and Dad Loudermilk *in the house!*" He fell out laughing and threw himself into my arms.

It was a long while before I pushed him away to get a good look at him, but why I bothered, I don't know, because as usual, nothing about him had changed. Nothing. He was thirty-two years old now, but Eddie still could have easily passed for a high school senior. And not just any senior—the senior Most Likely to Do the Nasty with Every Cheerleader on the Squad. You know the type I mean.

It's difficult for me to be objective about such things, of course, but I don't think it'd be stretching a point to say my son is a ladykiller. The physical evidence speaks for itself. He has the face of an angel and the grin of a mischievous child, and light amber eyes that can stop a girl's heartbeat at sixty paces. His skin is the color of tanned leather and as smooth to the touch as fine silk. Were it not for his height—he's only five foot eight—and his hair—he's lately taken to wearing it in a Rastafarian tumble of tight brown curls—he'd be too perfect to live. Trust me.

"Man, you look great!" he told me, beaming broadly. He'd grown a trim goatee since the last time we'd seen each other, and I liked it. I didn't want to, but I did.

He turned to his father. "Dad! What's up, man?" He shook Big Joe's hand vigorously and gave him a bear hug of his own. Joe remained stoic throughout.

"Damn, it's good to see you guys," Eddie said, releasing his father to consider us both at length.

"It's good to see you, too, baby," I said. "Isn't it, Joe?"

Eddie and I dug in and waited for my husband to say something.

"I don't know, yet," he grumbled after a while. It was really the most we could have hoped for.

Eddie looked at me and shrugged. "Same ol', same ol', huh?"

I just shrugged back at him.

The smile that had yet to leave his face widened again. "Hey, come on in and meet everybody," he said, ushering us through the door.

The inside of the house was just as beautiful as the outside, though it had the sparse appearance of a newlywed pair's first apartment. There was nothing hanging on the walls but white paint, and what furniture there was did little to break the monotony of the hardwood floors running through every room. All was clean and uncluttered, however, and that made up for a lot, in my book.

"Hey, everybody, they made it!" Eddie said as he turned his father and me into the living room, where two of his friends stood waiting. Two women, of course; I would have expected nothing else. Both roughly his age, late twenties to mid-thirties, and dressed in disparate variations of the standard college-kid uniform of blue denim and white cotton. One was barefoot, the other wore sandals, and they were both pretty. But that was where their similarities began and ended.

"Mom, Dad, this is Stacy and Eileen," Eddie said, waving the four of us together so that we might shake hands. The one he referred to as Eileen was the larger of the two, a curly-haired little blonde with a cute smile and a perfectly round face. She was working her way past pleasingly plump into too-overweight-for-her-own-good territory, but she didn't seem to have a problem with it; in fact, she seemed rather pleased with herself. As did the one named Stacy, though her high self-esteem was somewhat easier to understand: she was gorgeous. Raven-haired, olive-skinned, and shaped like someone who belonged on a postcard from Miami Beach.

"Hi," they both said cheerfully.

Big Joe was still shaking Stacy's hand a full two minutes later, apparently unable to extinguish the smile that had appeared from out of nowhere on his face.

"And the gourmet in the kitchen there is Angus," Eddie said, directing Joe's and my attention to a heavily bearded young man laboring over a hot stove off to our left. "As this is his house we're all crashing in, we thought it only fitting that he should do all the cooking in it. That's fair, right?"

"Ho, ho, ho," Angus said. He waved at us and said hello, then lifted a pot lid and bent over to inspect his handiwork. He was tall and thin, with arms and legs like soda straws, and his beard, a foot long if it was an inch, was rivaled in unruliness only by the hair on both sides of his head. What the man had against scissors and a comb, I couldn't begin to guess.

"How far away are we, doctor?" Eddie asked him.

"Fifteen minutes or so. This sauce is almost ready."

For the next half hour, the six of us waited the sauce out over drinks, making all the small talk hunger would allow. I was drinking Seven-Up, and Joe was doing beer. It was good to see him loosening up, but I knew that as the booze made him more sociable it was also going to make him less inhibited about speaking his mind, so I eavesdropped on his every word. Luckily, little of this preliminary conversation was of a political nature, and Joe was never really given any opportunity for debate.

That didn't come until dinner.

We had just sat down at the dining room table and begun to partake of the delectable baked chicken entrée Angus had prepared, when my husband looked directly at Eddie and said, "So what's the cause this time, Huey?"

He had asked the question as if it were an innocent one, but no one was fooled. Just as no one missed it as a veiled—and clearly irreverent—reference to Huey Newton, the former Black Panther leader.

"Excuse me?"

"Your cause. Your mission. What battle against the forces of evil are we waging today, here in Washington, D.C.?"

Eddie looked around at the rest of us, as if seeking our advice on how best to handle his father's boorish behavior. Finally, he just smiled and said, "We're here lobbying against the Meany Bill, Dad. Senator Dick Meany's proposed antidisclosure measure."

"Never heard of it," Joe said, as if proud of the fact.

"I didn't think you had."

"The Meany Bill, Mr. Loudermilk, if passed, would allow the federal government to deny any individual with a criminal record access to unclassified government files or documents pertaining to that individual," Eileen said.

"It's a direct affront to the Freedom of Information Act," Angus said.

"But if it only applies to criminals—" I started to say.

"Not criminals, Mom," Eddie said. "People with criminal records. There's a difference."

"We're not just talking about murderers and rapists here, Mrs. Loudermilk," Stacy said. "We're talking about anybody who has ever been arrested for, say, drunk driving.

Or marijuana possession. Or failure to pay alimony. Or—"

"Disturbing the peace," Eddie cut back in. "That would be a more relevant example. Because the real targets of this legislation are political dissidents. Otherwise known as liberals. Voices of the people who have dared to take an active role in the fight against social injustice in this country."

"Meany's selling the measure as a tool for tightening up national security," Eileen said, "but everyone knows that's just a smokescreen. What he's really looking to do here is close off the government's information highway to everyone on the left. He knows there isn't a political organizer worth his or her salt who's never been arrested for either staging or participating in a peaceful demonstration of some kind. Suspending the privileges of the Freedom of Information Act to anyone with a criminal record, no matter how innocuous that record may be, would effectively put all the locks back on the doors in Washington. The watchdog would no longer have any teeth."

"So you're here in D.C. to do what?" Big Joe asked, looking to Eddie specifically for an answer.

"We're here to get the word out, Dad," Eddie said. "To make sure the people know the truth about Senate Measure Eleven-Two-Oh-One before Senator Meany and his cronies can push it through."

"And how do you intend to do that? Get the word out, I mean?"

"By being everywhere Senator Meany goes in this town until the measure is voted upon," Angus said. "Every time he gets in front of a TV camera to sell that bill, we're going to be there to talk it down."

"And if talking doesn't work?"

Everyone just looked at him, including me. His inference was unmistakable, and no one knew quite how to respond to it.

"Joe—" I said.

"No, no! That's a fair question, isn't it? What are you kids gonna do if talking doesn't cut it? Say, the TV cameras won't stay on for you, or the newspaper reporters decline all your offers to hear your side?"

"Then we'll try other measures of protest," Stacy said calmly. There was a thread of iron in her voice I hadn't noticed before.

"Uh-huh. That's what I thought," Joe said. He started back on his dinner, effectively announcing the discussion over now that he'd finally heard what he'd wanted to hear.

"Joe, really!" I said. "You're being ridiculous. And insulting. These kids aren't the Weather Underground! They're just a group of young people who have taken an active interest in the affairs of their country."

"No, no, Mom, he's right," Eddie said angrily. "He's absolutely right. He's got us pegged. We're all *terrorists*. We've got a shitload of guns under every bed, and one of the bedrooms out back is a bomb factory. You wanna see it?" He got up from the table and waited. "Come on, I'll show it to you!"

"Eddie, please," Eileen said, her face reddening. "Don't."

"Joe, you apologize to our son and his friends immediately," I said. I could have strangled him.

"Apologize? For what? All I did was ask a question."

"All you did was insinuate that they don't know the difference between peaceful demonstration and guerrilla warfare."

"What?"

"Forget it, Mom," Eddie said. "What's the point? He'll never change."

"I'm not asking him to change. I'm asking him to apologize." I turned to Big Joe again. "Well?"

"Look, Eddie's right, Mrs. Loudermilk," Angus said. "This isn't necessary. We're all pretty thick-skinned around here, there's no harm done."

"Nonsense. He owes you an apology, and you're going to get one. Either that, or he's going to have a decision to make."

"What kind of decision?" Joe asked, a momentary glimmer of fear in his eyes.

"Where it is you want to sleep tonight," I said. "In the cab of our pickup, or outside in its bed?"

The room fell silent at the magnitude of my threat. Joe's lips moved, but he was unable to speak. Out of the corner of my eye, I saw Stacy lower her head and Eileen bring a hand up to cover her mouth.

If Joe wanted to accuse someone of terrorism, I was going to show him what real terrorism was.

"You've gotta be kidding," he said finally.

"Do I look like I'm kidding?" I asked him.

He examined my expression for a long minute, then started to chuckle. Before we knew it, he had us all cracking up. Even me.

"Hell, I'm sorry," he said when we'd all quieted down. "Dottie's right, I had no business talkin' to you kids like that."

Eddie's friends all made various noises and gestures of insouciance, going easier on him than I felt they had a right to.

"But you have to understand that, well . . ." He looked at Eddie. "I haven't always understood where Eddie was coming from."

Father and son held each other's gaze for an extended moment, making peace without words. The sight warmed my heart.

"We understand what you're saying perfectly, Mr. Loudermilk," Angus said. "We've all had similar communication problems with one or both of our parents, from time to time. We're used to it by now."

"But you really have nothing to worry about," Stacy said, smiling. "We're all pacifists. All of us believe non-violent demonstration is the only real way to effect permanent change in this country."

"All of us here, anyway," Eddie said. He and Stacy shared a curious, lingering glance.

"I suspect that was a veiled reference to me," someone outside the room said.

In the hallway near the front door stood another young man in his mid-to-late twenties, long-haired and goateed and dressed like a rapper on MTV. Which was to say his entire ensemble fit him like a parachute with sleeves. None of us had heard him come in. It was only a first impression, but the combination of his dress and posture as he stood there regarding us gave me the sense that this was a malcontent who not only dismissed the disapproval of others, but actively thrived upon it.

"Emmitt," Eileen said, with something that fell far short of enthusiasm.

"I was just gonna pick up my things and go, but if Eddie's gonna make me the center of conversation this evening, I may as well stick around and join the party, right?"

He started toward us.

"Nobody was talking about you, Emmitt," Stacy said. She was obviously disgusted.

"No? So who was he talking about, then? This traitor among us who thinks violence is the key to salvation?" He was standing toe-to-toe with Eddie now, staring him down. He was looking for a fight, and all of us could see it.

"Chill out, man," Eddie warned him. "This is not the

time or place, all right?'' He gestured toward Big Joe and me.

"Oh, right, right,'' Emmitt said, following Eddie's gaze. "Your folks are here tonight. Ma and Pa Loudermilk.'' To me, he said, "He tell you two the big news yet? He and Stacy are gonna be married.''

"Shut up, Emmitt!'' Stacy snapped.

"What? You mean marriage isn't in your plans?'' He looked at me again and smiled. "My mistake. Forget the marriage.'' And then to Stacy, with venom: "They're just screwing each other's brains out for the hell of it.''

Everyone at the table got on their feet at once, but Eddie had already thrown a punch by the time we did. Only Emmitt was able to do anything about it: He sidestepped Eddie's telegraphed right hand and produced a handgun from the waistband of his pants. Its flat, black nose was beneath Eddie's throat before anyone even recognized what it was.

"Ah-ah-ah, Eddie boy,'' Emmitt said. "You're a pacifist, remember? Violence is for us barbarians.''

"Jesus Christ, Emmitt, what are you doing?'' Angus cried.

"I'm defending myself, stupid. What does it look like I'm doing?''

"Emmitt, please. Don't do this,'' Stacy said.

"Don't do what? This asshole took a swing at me. You all saw it.''

"You're crazy, man,'' Eddie said, risking his life to state the obvious. "And if you don't get that gun outta my face right now—''

"Yeah?''

"Eddie!'' I shouted. "For heaven's sake, be quiet!''

"Listen to your momma, homeboy,'' Emmitt said. "You'll live longer.''

He started backing out of the room.

"Tell you what, Mouseketeers. You can keep my things as a going-away present. How's that?"

Eddie started after him, but Big Joe put a hand on his chest to stop him where he stood.

When Emmitt reached the front door, he shook his head sadly and said, "Why I hung with such a sorry bunch of losers as long as I did, I'll never know. But things are looking up. I'm about to make one hell of a splash in this town. You'll see."

If anybody wanted him to elaborate, no one said so; we all just wanted him gone.

And five seconds later, he was.

Angus was the first to break the silence that followed his departure. "Jesus," he said, mopping his brow with the back of one hand. He looked like he'd just stepped out of the shower and forgotten to towel off. "What the hell was he doing with a *gun*?"

"He's dead," Eddie said, livid. "I swear to God, he's dead."

"He's gone now, forget about him," Eileen said.

"I told you that sonofabitch was crazy! Didn't I tell you?"

"Eddie, baby, calm down," I said, moving to his side.

"He had no right to do that in front of you guys," he said, referring to his father and me. "He owes you more respect than that."

"I take it that used to be a friend of yours?" Big Joe asked.

"Used to be, yeah," Eileen said, when no one else would acknowledge the question. "But he's not anymore, as you can see. We broke off with him for good five days ago."

"Smart move."

"Of course, we would have done it sooner if some people had been less enamored with his archeorevolutionary

bullshit,'' Stacy said, cutting an accusatory glance at Angus.

"And just what the hell is that supposed to mean?"

"It means that egomaniacal psychopath would still be
one of the crew if you'd had your way. Wouldn't he?"

"Look. I never said we shouldn't send him on his way.
I only said we should give him a chance to clean up his
act first."

Eddie said something to dispute that, I don't recall what;
all I know is, it started a verbal free-for-all, and that was
it for our friendly little dinner party.

Big Joe and I took our dessert home in a box.

"You can say anything you want, Joseph Loudermilk,
just don't say 'I told you so.' "

"That boy Emmitt is certifiable. And up until five days
ago, he was part of the crowd Eddie's runnin' round with.
Now, maybe that doesn't sound like our son's become an
enemy of the people to you, but it sure as hell does to me."

"Joe, Eddie was the one who convinced the others to
expel him. They all admitted that."

"Of course he did. If I was doin' the wild thing with
another man's woman, I wouldn't want him around to complain about it either."

"Stacy is not Emmitt's woman."

"No. Not anymore, she isn't."

"Joe . . ."

"Jeez Looweez, woman, stop makin' excuses for the
boy. He's a hard-core militant who's fallen in with the
wrong people, and tonight it almost got him killed. Not to
mention us along with him."

Any answer I may have had for that never occurred to
me. Joe was making too much sense. A longer argument
on the way back to the trailer park would have helped to

pass the time, but my heart just wasn't in it. I wanted to believe Eddie's assertion that his problems with his friend Emmitt were strictly political, that he had extricated himself from the man's company simply because Emmitt's idea of political activism went beyond the pale, but no matter how hard I tried, I couldn't convince myself of that. Like Joe, I knew our son too well. Nine times out of ten, when Eddie failed to get along with another man, it had more to do with the man's wife or girlfriend than his ideals or moral character.

That night I went to bed clinging to the thought that, whatever the reasons for their parting of the ways, Emmitt was no longer an active member of Eddie's inner circle, and was never likely to be one again. It was the only encouraging note of the evening I could find. I had trouble sleeping all the same, but at least I was able to drop off eventually.

Not that I was out for long.

Come about four in the morning, Joe and I were awakened by the sound of someone drumming on Lucille's door. We both knew immediately it was bad news. It only takes a few months on the road in a trailer home to learn that a knock on your door in the wee hours of the morning is generally someone's way of informing you that the phone is ringing. For the rest of the world, this isn't necessarily cause for alarm; there's always the chance the person calling dialed the wrong number. Not so for trailer home owners. We don't receive calls made in error. Nobody comes to our door at four in the morning but the trailer park manager, and only because he or she has answered the park's phone and been told to wake us, specifically.

"Jeez Looweez," Joe mumbled, rolling out of bed before I could.

And yep, it was bad news.

He came back from the manager's trailer about ten minutes later, looking more tired than when he had left. I met him at the door, but he made me sit down before he would answer any of my questions.

At times like these, I always fear for my youngest first. I don't know why.

"Is it Theodore?" I asked Joe.

He shook his head. "No. It's Eddie."

"Oh, my God."

"No, no, he's fine. He's all right. He's just . . . in some trouble." He paused before going on. "Some big trouble."

I let him explain in his own good time.

"Emmitt's dead," he said at last. "And the police think Eddie murdered him."

2

If someone had told me the first official stop Joe and I would make on our long-awaited whirlwind tour of Washington, D.C., would be the District of Columbia courthouse building in the heart of downtown, I would have told them they were touched in the head. This was a city of infinite magic, loaded with history and teeming with excitement, where visitors ran out of time long before they ran out of places to go, or things to see. The fifteen museums of the Smithsonian Institution, the Pentagon building, the Kennedy Center, the Library of Congress, the Vietnam Veterans Memorial . . . The list of must-do's just goes on forever.

And there isn't a single courthouse on it.

You only start your stay with a courthouse if your last name is Loudermilk, and you've been lamebrained enough to time your visit to coincide with that of one of your screwball kids. In that case, knowing what you know about your children and the kind of luck they invariably visit upon you, you deserve whatever you get. It's the difference between merely getting hit by a truck and throwing yourself in front of one.

When was I going to learn?

For more than six hours that Tuesday, Big Joe and I sat glued to our seats in the crowded gallery of a madhouse known as Courtroom C10 and waited to catch a glimpse— the merest *glimpse*—of our incarcerated son. This was where he was to be brought before a magistrate and formally charged with murder, we were told, but no one could tell us exactly when this would occur; he could be the first prisoner brought before the judge today, or the ninety-seventh. As it happened, he was the forty-fourth. I know, because I counted.

The waiting had been torture, as one might expect, but actually seeing Eddie at last turned out to be much worse. Because seeing him was all I could do; they wouldn't let me talk to him. They wouldn't even let me near him. Joe and I had seen a day's worth of preceding cases go down, so we knew how brief his time in the room would be. The minute we saw him being escorted in, we both made a mad dash toward him, but it was no use. A bailiff stopped us dead in our tracks before we could reach so much as the gallery's railing, leaving us to shout and wail at the boy like mourners at a funeral.

The judge's gavel pounded, our silence was demanded, and then Eddie went the way of all the others before him: accused, charged, and sent off to jail. If you had blinked, you would have missed the whole thing.

"Mom, I didn't do it," Eddie said as they were leading him away.

Then he was gone again.

We had to wait until Wednesday morning to actually

speak with him. I have never had a longer Tuesday night in my life.

The first thing he said to me was a repeat: "Mom, I didn't do it."

The words took me back about thirteen months, to an equally disheartening moment in this mother's life, when another son faced the scrutiny of law enforcement officers who liked the way he fit into a murderer's shoes. The Loudermilk on the hot seat that time had been Theodore, my baby (or Bad Dog, as he's affectionately referred to by those of us who know and love him). It turned out in the end that his only crime had been showing up uninvited on our doorstep at Grand Canyon National Park at the exact same time a strange white man's corpse decided to appear in our bathroom, but for a while there it had looked like he was destined for a chain gang. The five days he spent trying to ease the suspicions of both his parents and the authorities in Arizona were five of the longest days I have ever known. However, he had never actually been arrested.

Imagine what I felt like now, just over a year later, watching a second child live the same nightmare, only worse. Eddie was an inmate at the District of Columbia Jail, and charges had been filed against him. Murder one, relative to the knifing death of one Emmitt Andrew Bell, the detectives we'd talked to the day before said, with not one ounce of doubt in their voices. They had already made up their minds.

"Tell us what happened," Big Joe said, once the three of us were alone in one of the jail's glass-lined visitation booths. Two years removed from the everyday life of a policeman, and he could still summon the imperturbable cool of one the instant it was needed.

"Dad, I don't know what happened. All I know is, somebody offed Emmitt Monday night, and the cops think it was me.''

Joe waited for him to go on, then said, ''And?''

''And what?''

''Did you?''

Eddie just sat there, stunned by the question.

''Come on, son. You understand what I'm asking. Did you kill the man?''

The hurt in Eddie's eyes quickly turned to anger. ''Now, do you think they would've found me sleepin' in my own damn bed that night if I'd killed the man, Dad?''

''Eddie, just answer the question.''

''No. Hell, no!'' Eddie said. He looked over at me. ''Mom . . .''

But I shook my head at him, refusing to take anything more than a minor role in his interrogation. I could play the Grand Inquisitor at home, but not here. Here, in this bar-lined room with its lifeless little windows and naked tables, Joe was the expert, not me, and I was smart enough to know it.

''Okay,'' Joe said. ''So you didn't kill him. Do you know who did?''

Eddie shook his head. ''No. I don't.''

''The police say they have witnesses who saw you two together Monday night at the nightclub where his body was found. Are you aware of that?''

''Yeah, I'm aware of it. So what?''

''So that puts you at the scene of the crime, boy. That's what.''

''So what if I was? Hell, man, those same witnesses saw me get up and leave, too. Emmitt was still alive and well when I walked out of there.''

''What time was this?''

''What time was what?''

"What time was it when you left the club?"

"I don't know." Eddie shrugged. "One-thirty, two o'clock, somethin' like that. I didn't pay any attention to the time."

Joe sighed deeply. "All right. Forget the time. What were you doing out there with Emmitt in the first place? The last time we saw you two, a reunion seemed like the last thing on your minds."

Eddie looked away for a second, then said, "He called the house lookin' for Stacy that night. Late." He showed us a little shrug of regret. "I happened to pick up the phone same time as she did. She was in the bedroom and I was in the kitchen, only I never let on I was there. I just stayed on the line and listened in, to hear what he was gonna say."

"And that was?"

"He gave her some line about wantin' to say good-bye. In person. Said he was leaving D.C. for good and he didn't want what happened at dinner Monday night to be the way she would remember him. Ain't that a laugh?"

"So he asked her to meet him at the club," Joe said, trying to keep him on track.

"Yeah. He made this big apology, then told her he'd only gone off like that because he'd had too much to smoke and drink. And of course, because he loved her." He smiled at the apparent irony of this last.

"You don't think he did, Eddie?" I asked him, finally breaking my extended silence.

"What? Love Stacy? Emmitt?" He laughed derisively. "Hell. You saw the man that night, Mom. He was crazy. Deranged. The boy didn't know up from down, and hadn't since the day I met him. How the hell was he gonna love somebody?"

"You don't have to be sane to be in love with someone, Eddie. In fact—"

Joe turned around and glared at me over his shoulder. Sometimes I think we've been together too long.

"You were saying Emmitt asked Stacy to come down to the club," Joe said, facing Eddie again.

"Yeah." Eddie nodded.

"Alone?"

"Yessir."

"But you wouldn't let her go."

"No, sir. The man was crazy, like I said, and he had a gun. You guys saw it. I told Stace she was nuts to even *think* about going over there."

"And yet, you went in her place."

Eddie didn't say anything.

"Did you go there to kill him, Eddie?" Joe asked, straight out.

"No. No way."

"But you said at dinner Monday night he was a dead man."

"Hey, Dad, come on. That was just a figure of speech, all right?"

Joe eyed him in silence.

"Look, I just wanted to make sure he understood that if he ever pulled a gun on me again, I was gonna feed it to him. Ass-end up. I went out there to deliver that message, and I did. That's *all* I did."

"So what was the knife for, then?"

"The knife?"

Joe expressed another heavy sigh. "The police say you were seen waving a nine-inch hunting knife in the man's face, Eddie."

"So I had a knife. He had a gun, right? What was I supposed to do, go over there and get in his face with nothin' but *air* in my hands?"

I closed my eyes and dropped my chin to my chest, asking the Lord for His help under my breath.

"Then you admit the knife they have is yours," Joe said.

"I admit it *looks* like mine. But that's all I admit."

"You don't know where your knife is?"

Eddie paused before answering. "No."

"And why is that?"

"Because I don't. It . . . I must've lost it somewhere."

"Lost it? Lost it where?"

"I told you, I don't know. At the club, I guess."

"During the fight."

"Waitaminute, waitaminute." Eddie waved both hands in front of his face to contest his father's last statement. "There was no 'fight,' okay? I don't care what those witnesses say. All we had was . . . an exchange of words."

Again, Joe's silence conveyed his skepticism.

"I flashed the knife, told him what I came there to tell him, and left," Eddie said. "The end."

"You're sure."

"Yes, I'm sure." He leaned forward toward his father, his temper flaring. "Look, Dad, this is bullshit, all right? The man was a raving lunatic. A Marxist basket case with delusions of grandeur. He kept talkin' about some deal he'd just made that was gonna blow the lid off of Washington and make him famous in the process. I got tired of hearing it, so I put him on his ass. One right hand, boom!—and then I was out of there. What happened to him out in the alley after that, I don't know, and I don't care."

"This big deal you just mentioned," I said. "He said something along those lines at the house Monday night, didn't he? Something about how he was going to make big news in this town, or—"

"Make a big splash," Joe said, recalling the remark. "He said he was going to make a big splash."

"Yes, that's right. He was going to make a big splash in this town, he said."

Eddie waited to see if we had a point to make. "So?"

Big Joe turned around and looked at me expectantly, essentially giving me the floor.

"So what was he talking about, exactly? Did he ever say?"

"Mom, who cares? I just told you, homeboy was *nuts*, it was all in his head."

"I'm sure it was. But humor me and tell me what he said anyway. Can you do that?"

My son opened his mouth to argue further, then caught sight of his father's face. End of argument.

"It had something to do with a book," he said, thoroughly disgruntled.

"A book?"

"Yeah. A book. The deal had somethin' to do with him buyin' a book, he said. Or *finding* a book. Buy, find . . ." He made a gesture with one hand to dismiss the significance of the distinction. "I don't remember which."

"He say what kind of book he was talking about?"

"No. 'Option,' that was the word he used. Option. He said he'd just optioned some book, but he didn't say what kind." When neither Joe nor I responded to that, he said, "Look, it was all bullshit, all right? I'm tellin' you guys. The man was all talk, the only two things he ever had goin' for him were his mouth and his imagination."

"And that was why you convinced your friends to show him the door. Because he had a big mouth," Joe said.

Eddie gave something away by not answering immediately. "That was part of it, yeah."

"And the other part?"

Our son said nothing, forcing Joe to answer his own question.

"And the other part was Stacy."

"Stacy?"

"That's right. Stacy. Please, boy, don't act stupid, all right? Your mother and I are not in the mood."

Eddie tried the waiting game again, but this time it wasn't going to work. When the ensuing silence became too much for him, he said, "So what's the question?"

"The question is, do the police have a right to believe you were nosing in on Emmitt's woman?"

"Stacy was never Emmitt's woman."

"No? He sure acted like she was last night."

"I told you. The fool was delusional. He had a crush on the girl, and she made the mistake of sleepin' with him once. One night in the sack, that's all they ever had together."

"But he took that to mean—"

"They had a thing goin'. Yeah."

"When the real 'thing' was between *you* and Stacy," I said.

Eddie shook his head again. "Uh-uh. Me an' Stace are just good friends, Mom, that's all."

"Who just happen to be 'screwing each other's brains out' every night," Joe said.

Eddie couldn't help but grin, never one to miss an opportunity to acknowledge a sexual conquest. "So we've been sleeping with each other every now and then. That supposed to make us engaged, or something?"

"No, but—"

"Look, Dad, we're wasting time. Are you gonna bail me outta here, or not?"

Joe looked at him for a long minute, and I did the same, a sure sign we had both lost all patience with him simultaneously.

"Bail you out?" Joe asked.

"Yes. Bail me out. This is a bullshit bust, I've got no business bein' in here!"

"Boy, you can't possibly be that stupid."

"Stupid?"

Joe was shaking his head at the floor.

"Eddie," I said firmly, "haven't you been paying attention? The judge denied bail for you yesterday, they're holding you on a *murder* charge."

"Yeah, but—"

"And for good reason, from what it sounds like to me," I added.

"Good reason?"

"Child, they've got you dead to rights. Everything seems to point to you. You aren't in here because they don't like the way you vote, you're in here because you're the perfect suspect."

"Bull—"

"And if you say that word one more time, I'll wear you out!"

"Listen to what your mother's tellin' you, boy," Joe said, finding his voice again. "She's tellin' you the truth. You're in serious trouble here, and all the knuckleheaded conspiracy theories in the world aren't gonna change that fact. So do us all a favor—stop cryin' foul and start defending yourself, all right?"

Eddie fell silent, too furious to speak. Joe and I just sat in our chairs and watched him bite his tongue, waiting to see where his anger would eventually take him. For Joe as well as me, it was like waiting for a despondent child to decide between leaping from the roof of a building or climbing down a fire escape to safety.

"Dad, I didn't do it," Eddie said at last, both sounding and appearing genuinely contrite. "I know it looks bad, but I didn't. I swear." He faced me. "I *swear*."

I nodded my head and smiled. "I know."

Eddie turned his gaze back to Joe.

"We both believe you," Joe said.

"We've already called your sister in California," I said, trying to sound excited about having involved Mo in all this. "She's trying to decide now whether to represent you herself or refer us to someone else in the area."

"I'll take the referral," Eddie said.

Mo had always treated him more like a son than a younger brother, and though they were close, her tendency to nag him about everything from his taste in clothes to his use of crude language generally drove him crazy.

"We'll see what we can do," I said as his father and I both stood up to leave.

He stood up too, and the guard who'd been watching us from his post on the other side of the booth's glass wall rushed in to get him, as if fearful Joe or I might try to smuggle our son out into the street in our clothing, or something.

"I didn't do it, Mom," Eddie said one more time. He sounded like a six-year-old.

"I know, baby," I said, choking back tears.

And, God bless him, Joe rushed me out before I could say anything more.

3

When I was done telling Mo the sad story, the first thing she said was, "I'm an adopted child, aren't I? Tell me the truth. You and Dad adopted me."

I told her I was sorry, but she was just as certifiable a Loudermilk as the rest of us.

"Mother, this is getting to be a habit with you two."

"I know. But what can I do?"

"For starters, you can forget you ever had any other children besides me. Stop taking my brothers' and sister's phone calls, and stop answering their letters. Maybe after a while they'll all just go away."

"Mo, that's terrible."

"No it's not. It's survival. Because if you and Daddy don't find a way to separate yourselves once and for all from these parasitic maniacs you gave birth to, you're going to die before your time. Both of you."

"Mo, your brother needs a lawyer, and he needs one fast.

I don't have time for lectures. Have you decided to handle his case or not?"

A long sigh traveled the length of the continent, from her phone in California to mine. "Mom, I would if I could," she said. "But I'm not a criminal lawyer, I'm a corporate litigations attorney. If I took Eddie's case, I'd probably just screw it up."

"I understand."

"But I have a call in to a specialist in town there who should be the perfect man for the job. As soon as he calls me back and I fill him in, I'll get you his number."

"Please, baby. Do that, will you?"

"Sure, Mom. Don't worry." She grew quiet all of a sudden. "Mom . . . you don't think there's any chance he actually did it, do you?"

In the thirty-something hours since I'd first learned of the crime Eddie was accused of, I had asked myself this very question over a thousand times, and still I had no single answer for it.

"I don't think so, Mo," I said. "I believe I know your brother better than that. But . . . you know how he can be sometimes. When he's pushed into a corner . . ."

"Except that he wasn't pushed into any corner, from what you just told me. Was he? I mean, this Emmitt didn't come looking for Eddie, Eddie came looking for him."

"That's what they tell us, yes."

"Then the question isn't whether or not Eddie's capable of killing someone in the heat of an argument. The question is, is he capable of killing someone *after* the argument is over?"

I gave that some thought, then shook my head at no one and said, "My answer would still be no. Absolutely not. I don't think Eddie could kill anyone under *any* circumstances, and neither does your father."

"Good. I feel the same way."

"Then let's hurry up and get your brother out of that awful jail, shall we?"

"I'm placing another call to my friend now, Mother."

"Very good, baby. Call us at the trailer park as soon as you hear something."

I hung up the phone without saying good-bye.

"There it is! The Washington Monument! Did you see it?"

I pointed out my window at an ambiguous white obelisk that kept bobbing in and out of our view above the city's skyline.

Joe's eyes never wavered from the road ahead.

And who could blame him? Catching glimpses of the spires and domes of Washington's taller buildings from the windows of a moving pickup truck was no way to see the sights of the nation's capital, but to this point, that was all either of us had had time for. It was depressing enough for me, but for Joe it was nothing less than devastating. The city of his dreams, and all he could do was flit about it like a fly. He couldn't have been more demoralized had he been a child handcuffed to a lamppost at Disneyland.

And of course, he was worried about Eddie, too. The argument he had made for returning to Lucille at the trailer park when I'd suggested we go have a talk with Eddie's friends was strictly for show; he was no more willing to entrust our son's fate to the local authorities than I was. But we had crossed paths with Eddie in the first place over his strenuous objections, and pretending to want nothing more to do with our son or his problems was Joe's way of saying I had stuck my foot in it again.

When we arrived at the brownstone in Dupont Circle where we'd dined two nights before, only Stacy and Eileen

were at home. Angus, they said, was out shopping somewhere. Eileen met us at the door. She looked tired and
distraught, and had little to offer in the way of a greeting.
Stacy, on the other hand, seemed more sullen than anything
else; the frown she wore carried as much impatience as it
did concern. And if she felt any sympathy for Joe and me
at all, she never mentioned it.

When we all settled uneasily into the living room, I asked
the pair what they knew about Emmitt's death. For now at
least, Joe was content to let me lead this particular parade.

"Only what the police have told us," Eileen said. "They
say Eddie killed him Monday night. At some club out in
Logan Circle."

"And you believe that?" I asked.

Eileen turned her head to consult with Stacy before answering, but Stacy was of no help to her; only her eyes
betrayed the fact that she was aware of Eileen at all.

"Well, *I* don't," Eileen said in time.

"What about you?" I asked Stacy.

"I don't know what I believe, Mrs. Loudermilk," she
said.

"You mean to say you actually think Eddie might have
done such a thing?"

She opened her mouth to answer, only to stop and re-
consider. By the time she finally spoke, her expression had
softened and there was less of an edge to her voice. "Look.
I know you're Eddie's mother, and you probably think you
know him pretty well, but . . . you haven't been around him
much lately, like Eileen and I have. And while he's a really
good person at heart, he . . . he has a dark side you and
your husband have probably never even seen."

"A dark side? What kind of dark side?"

Again, she hesitated before answering. "He has a temper, Mrs. Loudermilk. A really *bad* temper. And when he

thinks somebody hasn't shown him the respect he deserves, he can get a little . . . crazy.'' She shrugged, as if that would make her meaning clear.

"Eddie has always had a temper," Big Joe said. "But he's never been one to let it get the better of him. Certainly not to the point of killing somebody. Sure, he's gotten in some scrapes and scuffles with people, but he's never been moved to hurt anybody seriously. He's too smart for that."

Eileen and Stacy's mutual silence made for a ringing note of dissent.

"You don't agree?" Big Joe asked them.

Stacy was content to remain silent, but Eileen broke down and said, "It's not that we don't think Eddie's smart, Mr. Loudermilk. It's just that . . ."

"What?"

"Well, we've seen him go off on people before."

"Explain 'go off,' " I said.

"Well . . ." She thought a moment. "We've never known him to use a knife on anybody before, but . . . there was this guy out at Rock Creek Park, once. A long-haired redneck, crazy drunk and big. There was a jazz concert going on at the amphitheater and we were all passing out fliers to the crowd. This guy got upset and started slapping them out of our hands. First Angus, then me and Stacy. Eddie and Emmitt were on the other side of the theater.

"Eddie raced over when he saw what was happening and jumped all over the guy. He was shoving fliers down his throat before any of us could move. By the time we pulled him off—"

"Waitaminute, waitaminute," Big Joe said. "What happened before that?"

"Before?"

"Before Eddie jumped him. Eddie wouldn't have attacked somebody just for knocking a bunch of fliers out of his friends' hands. He would have needed more provocation than that.''

"Like what?" Eileen asked.

"Like being called out of his name, for instance.''

"Out of his name?''

"He means something racist," Stacy said, understanding immediately.

"Yes," Joe said.

"You want to know if the man called Eddie a nigger. Is that it, Mr. Loudermilk?''

"Yes. That's exactly what I'm asking.''

Why hadn't I thought of that myself? I wondered. Eddie's hatred for the dreaded *n* word was legendary in the Loudermilk household. As long as I could remember, it had affected him like a backhand slap to the face. Over the years, a great many black Americans had learned to tolerate the slur's utterance with a dignified indifference, but Eddie had never been one of those people, and seemed to have no wish to become one. He was a young man with a short fuse under the best of circumstances, but nothing could light a fire under him faster than being called a nigger to his face.

"Of course," Stacy said.

"That's what I thought.''

"But . . . what difference does that make?''

"What do you mean?''

"I mean, what difference does it make *what* sets Eddie off? The point Eileen and I were trying to make is that he *can* be moved to violence. What does it matter how he gets there?''

Joe had no answer for that, and neither did I.

"So Emmitt provoked him. So what? Words are just words, Mr. Loudermilk. You can tune them out if you don't want to hear them. But you men aren't very good at that, are you?"

"Stacy . . ." Eileen said.

Stacy turned, eyes flashing, but took the hint and said no more.

"Tell us about Emmitt," Joe said, adroitly changing the subject to keep the two women engaged in the conversation.

"What about him?" Eileen asked.

"How did he end up on the outs with the rest of you? Something must have happened to make you all turn on him like you did."

"We didn't turn on him. We just . . . didn't see eye to eye on things anymore."

"What kind of things?"

"You said you talked to Eddie this morning," Stacy said. "Surely he must have told you."

"He told us what *his* problems were with Emmitt, yes. But not yours."

Just when it seemed neither woman was going to respond to that, Eileen said, "Some of us thought, as Eddie did, that Emmitt was getting dangerous. He was . . . starting to get some crazy ideas about political reform and how to achieve it, and it made us a little uneasy. So . . . after some discussion, we agreed it might be best if Emmitt went his way and we went ours."

"After some discussion," Joe repeated.

"Yes, sir."

"You mean there was some debate about it."

"Yes."

"And Eddie was his primary detractor."

Eileen nodded.

"Who were Emmitt's defenders?"

"Well, me, for one," Eileen admitted, getting the words

out quickly before she could lose the nerve. "And Angus, for another. We both liked Emmitt, and had a hard time seeing him as Eddie and Stacy did. In fact, I thought they might . . . have some ulterior motive for wanting Emmitt to leave." She cut a very brief glance in Stacy's direction, then said, "But eventually, I came to understand that wasn't the case at all. Emmitt really was out of control, just like they said, and we needed to do something about him before somebody got hurt."

"You saw what he was like Monday night," Stacy said. "He was insane. You couldn't reason with him anymore. We knew we were headed for trouble if we all stayed together, so we tried to head things off by breaking up. I guess we just didn't do it in time." Without intending to, she'd made this last sound like a personal apology.

"Then Emmitt's problems with all of you were strictly political," I said.

"No. Of course not. Eddie must have told you that Emmitt was jealous, too. Of me and Eddie. He had no right to be, but that was beside the point."

"He had no right to be jealous?"

"No. He didn't."

"Why was that?"

"Because there was nothing between me and Eddie. There's nothing between me and anyone. There never has been. Emmitt had no claim on me, and neither does Eddie. The difference is, Eddie has always understood that, and been cool with it. But not Emmitt."

"Eddie was never jealous of Emmitt?" Big Joe asked.

"Eddie jealous? Of Emmitt?" She smiled. "Not hardly."

Joe turned back to Eileen. "You said Angus was Emmitt's other defender."

"That's right." She nodded her head.

"But that he came around to seeing Emmitt the way Eddie and Stacy did, eventually. Just like you did."

"No. I never said that."

That caught Joe a little by surprise. "You mean he never did change his mind about Emmitt?"

"Not completely, no. He and Emmitt were old school buddies. They went to Michigan State together. It was Angus who brought Emmitt into the fold. He thought highly of Emmitt, and probably still does. He only went along with our decision to ask Emmitt to leave because he could see there was no use arguing about it anymore. Once I went over to the other side, he was the only one fighting for Emmitt to stay, and I guess he just got tired of that after a while."

"Was Angus angry about Emmitt being forced to leave?" I asked.

When Eileen took too long to answer that, Stacy said, "Yes."

"Was he angry at anyone in particular?"

"You mean, was he angry at Eddie?"

"For turning the rest of you against Emmitt, yes."

Stacy paused indecisively, then said, "Yes. He was."

"Pardon me for asking, Mrs. Loudermilk," Eileen broke in, "but why are you and your husband asking all these questions? I mean, what's the point?"

"The point," I said, before Joe could get his mouth open to answer the question first, "is that Mr. Loudermilk and I don't have the problem you and Stacy seem to have where Eddie is concerned. We have no doubts about his being innocent of Emmitt's murder. None whatsoever. So we are going to do whatever it takes to get him out of that jail as soon as possible. Even if that means we have to find Emmitt's real murderer ourselves."

"Dottie . . ." Joe said, sensing a storm brewing.

"No, no, the child asked us a question, and I'm going to answer it," I said, riding a roll of emotion I didn't realize had been building up inside me until this moment. Still glaring at Eileen, I said, "You think we should just let the police handle things, is that it? Just get out of the way and let the professionals do their job?"

"Well—" Eileen started to answer.

"To hell with that, little girl. That's my child they've got locked up in that jail cell, and I'm not trusting anybody to get him out but me. Me and his father."

"Mrs. Loudermilk, please. I didn't mean to suggest—"

"You call yourselves the boy's friends, but you have no faith in him. You don't *know* him. You think because he can become hotheaded at times, he's capable of knifing a man to death. Over an *insult*."

"We didn't say that."

"No. But you haven't said any different, either, and to me that's worse. No wonder the police are so certain the boy is guilty. With you two backing him up, he must look like the second coming of Attila the Hun."

"Dottie, stop it!" Joe said, using the one tone of voice I've never been able to ignore. It's the one he always uses whenever I've just done something he knows I'm going to regret the following morning. "You're getting a little carried away now."

Of course, he was right, and I knew it immediately. I felt like an old fool who'd just been found walking in circles on a neighbor's lawn, ranting and raving at the moon.

"I'm sorry," I said, to no one and everyone. "I must be losing my mind."

Before a difficult silence could fully entrench itself in the room, Stacy stood up and said, "Let me go get you some water."

She came back from the kitchen with a full glass, and I

sipped at it gingerly, trying to give myself all the time I needed to return to my senses.

"You're right, Mrs. Loudermilk," Stacy said. "We have been prejudging Eddie. I don't know why, but we have."

"If you could have seen how he and Emmitt have been treating each other lately . . ." Eileen said.

"I guess what it boils down to is, we've been *expecting* them to kill each other. So when the police showed up yesterday and said Emmitt was dead . . ."

"I understand," I said.

"No. We owe you an apology," Eileen said. "And Eddie, too. He *is* our friend, and as such, he deserves the benefit of the doubt."

Stacy nodded her head at me to show that she agreed.

"All the same, I shouldn't have torn into you two like that," I said. "I'm sorry."

"Don't be," Stacy said.

"If you have any more questions, go ahead and ask them," Eileen said, looking at Joe. "If you think it'll help Eddie, we'll tell you anything you want to know."

Joe studied me and I studied him. The slight nod I gave him was both to let him know I was okay, and to defer the rest of the questioning to him.

"All right," he said, facing the girls again. "Let's get back to Emmitt." Hearing no objections, he went on: "You said at dinner the other night it had been five days since the four of you put him out. Is that right?"

Eileen glanced at Stacy, then said, "Yes. We told him to leave last Monday, and by Wednesday, he was gone. I don't think any of us had seen him since then until Monday night."

I thought I saw Stacy about to second that, but all she did was shift her weight around in her chair.

"Then he'd been staying somewhere else for at least five days," Joe said.

"Yes," Eileen replied.

"Did he say where he was going? Or who, if anyone, he intended to stay with?"

Eileen shook her head vigorously, but Stacy said, "I don't know for sure, but . . . I might have an idea." When all eyes turned to her, she said, somewhat sheepishly, "I went to see him Saturday afternoon. At someone's apartment out in Georgetown."

Eileen's jaw dropped open.

"Whose apartment?" Joe asked.

"I don't know," Stacy said. "He never said."

"He never said?"

"No. And I never asked. I guess I should have, but I didn't."

"But you could tell it was someone else's apartment?"

"Yes. It had to be. The place was fully furnished, and it looked lived in. You know—food in all the cupboards, and clothes hanging everywhere."

"Men's clothing, or women's clothing?"

"Men's clothing. At least, that's all I could see. I didn't look in the closets or anything."

"He was there alone?"

"Yes."

"What did he want to see you about?"

Stacy thought her answer through before delivering it. "He wanted to talk about us. Me and him. It was the same old thing. And of course, he wanted money. Emmitt always wanted money."

"Money?"

"Yeah. Ask Eileen. Begging for money was Emmitt's primary occupation."

"How much did he want?"

"Well, that was the unusual part. He wanted five hundred dollars."

"Five hundred dollars?" Eileen cried.

"Yeah. Isn't that wild?" To Joe, she said, "See, Emmitt never used to think that big. His needs weren't that great. He'd ask you for a few dollars to pay for his next meal, and that was it. When he asked me for five hundred bucks, I figured it could only be for one thing: to help him find a place of his own. But when I asked him about it, he said he needed the money—"

"To buy a book," I said, making a calculated guess out loud.

Stacy's eyes opened wide. "That's right. That's exactly what he said. He needed it to buy a book. But—"

"Did he say what kind of book?" Joe cut in, demanding her attention again before she could get too caught up in the wonder of my clairvoyance.

"What kind?"

"Yes. What kind. What kind of book was he talking about?"

She shook her head. "I don't know. He wouldn't say. I asked him, but he wouldn't tell me."

Joe and I let out a collective sigh, disheartened. It seemed that everyone knew that a book of some kind had been one of the last things on Emmitt's mind before his death, but no one could tell us its title. Or the nature of its text. Was it a big book, or a small book? A hardback, or a paperback? Did it belong in someone's study on a shelf, or in their bathroom atop the dirty-clothes hamper?

Nobody knew.

"Did you give him the money?" Joe asked, bravely forging on.

"What? To buy a book he wouldn't tell me anything about? Are you kidding? I told him I was sorry, but I

couldn't help him. Then I wished him good luck and left."
She stopped to brush a strand of hair away from her face.
"I didn't see him again until Monday, when he broke in
here and made such a mess of dinner."

"He didn't actually break in," Eileen corrected. "He
still had a key."

"He did?" Joe asked.

"Sure. We would have asked him for it last Wednesday,
except that he hadn't completely moved out yet. That was
why he came over Monday, remember? To pick up the last
of his things."

I looked back on Emmitt's interruption of our dinner two
nights before and recalled that she was right: Before he and
Eddie went after each other, he had indeed said something
about being there to "pick up his things."

I also recalled something else.

"Where are his things now?" I asked Eileen.

"Where are they?" The question seemed to throw her.
"I just told you. He . . ." And then *she* remembered.
"Oh!"

"He never took them," Stacy said, following our lead.
"He left without them that night. They must still be back
in his room."

"Yes," I said.

"We'd like to see what he left behind, if you don't
mind," Joe said, standing up. "We won't take anything, of
course. We just want to look."

Stacy stood up herself and shrugged. "Sure. Why not?"

Eileen waited until the last minute to follow us out of
the room.

Emmitt's bedroom was down in the basement, and the
last of us hadn't stepped off the stairs when we knew something about it wasn't right. It was a mess. The kind of mess
searches leave behind, not slovenly housekeepers. For the

most part, the room was bare—just a double bed, one night-stand, and a small chest of drawers; exactly what one might have expected Emmitt to leave behind upon moving out. Except that it was all turned upside down. Not in a hap-hazard way, oddly enough, but with obvious care. Things had been moved and upended, yes, but not tossed aside or dumped unceremoniously. Newspapers and clothing, lamp-shades and shoes—all had been displaced, but not abused. It was amazing.

A humane vandalism.

"Oh, my God," Eileen said.

"Somebody's been in here," Stacy said, sounding shaken. "Look at this place!"

"Oh, my God," Eileen said again.

"When were you in here last?" Big Joe asked them.

Apparently, neither woman heard the question.

"I said, when were you in here last?"

Stacy spun around, returning to the real world. "Oh. *I* was in here yesterday. Looking for a pair of sunglasses."

"And the room was okay then?"

"Okay? Yes, yes. The room was okay then."

"Then this must have happened last night."

Stacy shrugged. "I guess so. Yes." She turned to Eileen. "But we didn't hear anything. Did we?"

"You probably weren't meant to," Big Joe said. "That's why things look the way they do in here. Whoever did this was trying to be quiet."

"But how did they get in?" Eileen asked. She appeared to be on the verge of tears.

Joe's eyes scanned the room for a moment; then he pointed a finger at a far wall. "Through there. See?"

One of the large basement windows was swung fully open, only the smallest shards of glass left mounted in its frame.

"Oh, my God," Eileen said for the third time.

Joe surveyed the room once more and finally said, "I take it Emmitt's things are gone."

Stacy walked about, eyeing the floor, then nodded. "As a matter of fact, Mr. Loudermilk, they are."

Eileen was the only one on the premises who seemed the least bit surprised.

___ 4 __

The lawyer Mo eventually found for Eddie was a mellif-luously nice white man named Kostrzewski. Arthur Kos-trzewski. Mo said they had met at a legal seminar of some sort in Denver, Colorado, three years earlier, and had quickly become friends. All they did the whole weekend was flash pictures of their families and trade one-liners about the stifling boredom of the event. Afterward, they'd exchanged business cards and promised to keep in touch, but of course, neither had.

I had never known Mo to be unfaithful to her husband B.C., so incredibly idyllic was their marriage, yet I couldn't help but wonder if there wasn't more to her relationship with Kostrzewski than she was telling. After all, from the sound of it, the circumstances of their meeting were ripe with opportunity for an affair, and since they supposedly got such a kick out of each other's company . . . Well, let's just say I had my doubts.

Until I met the man.

The Pillsbury Doughboy on Valium. Same bulbous cheeks, same black-button eyes, same general unhealthy pallor: white on white, with a dash of Gold Medal flour for color. Replace the baker's cap on the biscuit pitchman's head with a hefty portion of straight black hair, and that was Kostrzewski. Only Kostrzewski was more cheerful. To get a chuckle out of the doughboy, you had to give him a good stiff poke in the belly; Kostrzewski required no such inducements. He was the most happy-go-lucky attorney I'd ever seen.

But Mo said he was our man, so Joe and I retained his services. We met him over coffee early Wednesday afternoon, about two hours after leaving Stacy and Eileen in Angus's burglarized brownstone, at a small café on Pennsylvania Avenue Northwest, less than three blocks east of the White House. We told him everything we knew about Eddie's case and then answered the half-dozen or so questions he had for us afterward. The man laughed and smiled cheerfully throughout.

By the time he left us to go talk to Eddie himself, I felt like I'd been trapped in an amusement-park fun house for a week and ten days.

"I hope your daughter knows what she's doing," Joe said as we walked back to our truck. We'd deliberately parked it blocks away from the café so that we'd have no choice but to at least get a fleeting glimpse of the White House today, if nothing else.

And after a moment, there it was. The Presidential Palace. Unmistakable, yet somehow unspectacular. As viewed from the front—the side that faced Pennsylvania Avenue—it looked surprisingly small; like an oversized dollhouse someone had planted at the far end of the grounds beyond the black iron gates ringing the perimeter. Of course, it was distance that created this illusion; on this side of the building, over two hundred yards of flawless White House lawn stood between it and the street. Still, it was a special sight, out of scale or not. The playground of kings and queens, movie stars and Nobel Prize winners; a shrine to history made, and history yet to come. The White House.

"Jeez Looweez," Joe said.

He was speaking for us both.

"Understand something right now," Big Joe said. "After this, we're through. The boy's got a lawyer now, we don't have to do this anymore."

"I hear you," I said.

"I mean it, Dottie. This is our last stop. Mr. Kostrzewski takes over from here on in."

"All right, baby. Whatever you say."

It was easy to acquiesce now; I'd gotten what I wanted. Instead of going back to the trailer park and spending the rest of the day and night inside Lucille, we had driven out to Georgetown to find the apartment Stacy had allegedly met Emmitt in the Saturday before. I'd made her tear her room apart in search of an address, and by some stroke of good fortune, she'd managed to find one.

Georgetown was a charming neighborhood, but in a well-worn sort of way. At least, this was true of its southernmost hemisphere—near the Georgetown University campus—where our business had taken us. Here, its architectural flavor was much the same as that of Dupont Circle, only without all the fresh paint and newly poured concrete. In contrast to the elegant north end of town, which we had yet to see, this end looked a little tired; or, more to the point, comfortably used, like a pair of old shoes you'd throw away if they didn't feel so good on your feet. A perfect personality for a college town, I thought.

The building we were looking for fit right in with this
quiet, unassuming motif. On a tree-lined stretch of Thirty-
second Street, just three units north of Prospect, stood a
two-story Victorian row house, white with black trim and
dappled in shade. A low-slung white picket fence separated
a yard filled with dry grass and yellow leaves from the
cobblestone sidewalk out front. If anyone was at home inside, they were viewing the world through closed blinds
and curtains at all the windows.

We parked the truck across the street and I led the way
to the door, Joe trailing just behind. At least, he was until
I heard him grumble about something and turned to see that
he had stopped. He was scraping his left foot on the grass
along the walkway near the fence; apparently, he had
stepped in something brown and wet, and was cursing the
gods for having left it in his path. I just shook my head
and went on without him. I raised my right hand to knock
on the door . . .

. . . when I noticed it was ajar.

I turned back to Joe, but he was still busy worrying about
the state of his shoe. I thought about waiting until he was
finished and by my side again to do or say anything more,
but that was a short-lived thought better suited to someone
less bold—and impulsive—than I. I pushed the door open
and stepped inside.

"Hello?"

A flash of movement immediately drew my eyes to the
right, where a man stood frozen in an open doorway, returning my startled gaze with one of his own. He was a
short, clean-shaven white man in a blue silk suit, with a
dimpled chin and a balding pate marred only by a single
tuft of brown hair that rose above his forehead like a uni-
corn's horn.

And he was gone before I could blink.

He was gone so fast, in fact, that it took me a full minute to decide he'd been real, and not something I'd imagined. When my feet were at last ready to move, I called out to Joe and, again without waiting for him to join me, rushed to the doorway where the stranger had stood—only to find myself staring into an empty kitchen and the back door swinging open beyond it.

"What the hell's goin' on?" Big Joe asked, finally catching up with me again. "You okay?"

I took a deep breath and nodded. "I think so."

"What happened? One minute, you're knockin' on the door, and the next—"

"I didn't knock on the door. It was open. I just pushed it open and came in. And then . . ."

He let me tell it at my own pace.

"And then I saw someone. He was standing right here, right where we're standing now."

"It was a man?"

"Yes. It was a man. He was dressed in a blue suit, and he had this little patch of hair sticking up out of the top of his head . . ." I tried to show him where it was.

"So where is he now?" He peered into the kitchen again and noted the open back door. "Out there?"

"Yes. At least, I guess that's where he went. He saw me come in and took off like a shot."

Before I could stop him, Joe walked slowly through the kitchen and the service porch beyond it to the back door, where he stuck his head out the open portal to take a look around. He was careful about it, but that didn't stop me from worrying; Joe's head was a mighty big target.

"No one out here," he said eventually. He closed the door and started back toward me.

He walked to the front door and inspected the lock and jamb. "This was jimmied," he said.

"I told you."

"We'd better call the police. You see a phone some-where?"

I surveyed the room. A tiny living room sparsely filled with cheap furniture and, just as Stacy had said, liberally sprinkled with male clothing. In fact, I could see a phone cord running up under a pair of patterned shorts sprawled out on the floor.

"Not in here," I lied.

"Never mind. We can call from a pay phone. Come on." Joe stepped out onto the porch and waved at me to follow.

"Joe, we can't go now," I said.

"Oh yes we can. This is a crime scene, Dottie. Your friend in the blue suit was a burglar. And we can't go around touching things in here—"

I turned my back on him and said, "We're not going to touch anything. We're just going to look. I promise."

I saw a hallway off to my left and headed for it.

"Dottie!"

The first door on the left was a bathroom. The first door on the right was a small bedroom that had been converted into a study. It was just big enough to hold a small couch and a circular coffee table, the former set at one end of the room opposite a wall lined with books. Or, more accurately, a wall lined with book*shelves*. Empty bookshelves.

Because all the books were on the floor. And on the couch. And on the coffee table. It looked like someone had dropped them en masse from the ceiling.

"Dottie, I told you—"

Joe had raced in after me and was reaching for my arm when he caught sight of the little study over my shoulder.

"Do you see what I see?" I asked him.

He didn't say anything.

"Books. All he touched were books."

"That's all he touched in this room. We don't know what the rest of the place looks like, and we're not gonna find out. We're getting out of here, Dottie. Right now."

"But Joe—"

"But Joe, nothing. Let's go." He took my arm and gently pulled me away.

We turned in the hallway to leave and nearly slammed into a young man standing there, shaking like a half-nude sorority girl in a slasher movie.

"We didn't do this," Joe assured him.

"Of course not," the young man said. It seemed what he had in mind was to patronize and backpedal at the same time.

"Please. You have to believe us," I said. "The man who broke in here was already inside when we arrived."

He stopped moving backward. He looked to be in his early twenties, with huge blue eyes and long blond hair that ran from the edge of an expansive forehead all the way down to his shoulders. "What man?" he asked.

I told him about the well-dressed interloper I'd caught standing in his kitchen door. His reaction to the news was either very well masked or entirely nonexistent.

"So who are you?" he asked next. He didn't look afraid anymore.

"That's a long story," I said.

"So? You've got time. It's gonna take the cops at least twenty minutes to get here."

Without bothering to ask if we had any objections, he left us to use the phone.

He took word of Emmitt's death hard.

"Well, that solves that problem," he said. "I'd been wondering how I was going to get him out of here."

He said his name was Curtis Howell, and that he and

Emmitt had met three months ago at a revival movie theater in town called the Alexandria. There'd been a Hitchcock double feature showing that night, and the two men had struck up a conversation relative to the strengths and weaknesses of *Strangers on a Train* while standing in line for the snack bar. The conversation had continued at a coffee shop afterward, where addresses and phone numbers had been exchanged. They had seen each other only once more after that, at the theater again, until Emmitt showed up at Curtis's door last Friday, looking for a place to "crash" for a few days. He'd slept on a bus bench the two nights previous, he said, and he didn't have a third night in him.

"I don't know what made me tell him he could stay," Curtis said. "I must have been crazy. He was a nice enough guy, and he had a good sense of film, but that's no reason to allow someone as basically rude as Emmitt was into your home."

He not only insisted that he didn't know anyone that resembled the man I'd scared out of his home, he claimed not to know anyone who owned a blue suit. And when he heard about my suspicion that this formally attired burglar had only been interested in his books, he left us in the living room to go check, his eyes alight with curiosity.

Less than a minute later, he was back.

"I don't believe it, but you're right. He didn't touch a thing but my books. Went through every one in the house."

"Did he take anything?" Big Joe asked.

"I don't know. It's hard to say. I haven't had time to go through them all yet." He thought a moment. "You say this guy was looking for a book of Emmitt's?"

"That's our guess. Did Emmitt have any books with him?"

"I don't remember seeing any. They would have been among his things, if he had."

"His things?"

"Yeah. You know—his luggage. His bag."

"What kind of bag?"

"An overnight bag. A black leather overnight bag. It's in his room, if you want to see it."

It was full of clothes and little else. Underwear, T-shirts, socks, two pair of Levi's, and assorted toiletries. It was zipped closed when we found it, its contents seemingly undisturbed.

"I didn't think he had any books with him," Curtis said.

"Maybe he talked about them instead," Joe said.

"Excuse me? Oh." Curtis shook his head. "Not with me he didn't. Emmitt and I talked about movies, TV, politics— but no books. Sorry."

"Did you know our son Eddie?" I asked.

"No, ma'am. I didn't know any of Emmitt's other friends. All I knew about any of them was what he told me."

"Then he never had guests here, that you're aware of," Joe said.

"No, sir. At least, I don't think he did. It's hard to say what he did in here while I was at school."

Joe and I exchanged a glance, deciding without words that there'd be little point in telling him about Stacy's visit to his home Saturday.

"What about phone calls?" Joe asked.

"You mean, did he make any?"

"Or receive any. Yes."

"Sure. I don't know how many, but he used the phone quite a bit, yes."

"Could you tell who he was talking to?"

"Not really. I was usually in the other room. But I do remember answering the phone once and having someone ask for him. He said his name was Vlade."

"Vlade?"

"Yeah. At least, that's what it sounded like he said. And when I told Emmitt it was Vlade calling, he seemed to recognize the name."

"That's Vlade, V-L-A-D-E, like in Vlade Divac?"

"Who's Vlade Divac?"

"He plays center for the Lakers," I said.

(See, this is how it works: We wives spend years picking up bits and pieces of senseless sports data from our ESPN-loving husbands, thinking it will never be put to good use . . . and then, one day, it happens. The perfect opportunity arises for us to expel some of it. A question is asked you have no interest in hearing, let alone answering, and out of your mouth pops a name, or a date, or a batting average you had no idea you even knew. Or a team name and position played. Today, Vlade Divac; tomorrow, Cecil Fielder.)

"Never heard of him," Curtis said.

It seemed he didn't know very much at all. He didn't know Emmitt's friends, he didn't know anything about this book business, and he didn't know the man in the blue suit who'd broken into his apartment. And worse, he didn't act like he cared to know.

Perhaps reaching this same conclusion himself, my husband looked at his watch and said, "Look, Curtis. Would you care to do the wife and me a big favor?"

A cloud of suspicion came over the young man's face. "What kind of favor?" he asked.

"Let us walk out of here. Right now, before the police arrive."

Curtis just stared at him, unsure of what to say.

"We didn't have anything to do with your break-in here. You believe that, don't you?"

"Well . . ."

"If we're still here when the cops show up, they aren't likely to arrest us, but they'll keep us downtown answering questions for days. And we don't have that kind of time, as we said before. We have a son in jail who needs our help."

"Yes, but—"

"And they won't just tie *us* up answering questions. They'll grill you for days too."

"Me? Why me?"

"Because our story's not going to make any sense. And when the police are confronted with a story that makes no sense, they don't stop asking questions until it does. Believe me."

"On the other hand," I said, "if you'll just let us go . . ."

"They'll take your statement and leave. All you have to tell them is that you found the man Dottie described in your house when you came home, and that he ran off. What do you say?"

Curtis eyed the two of us in silence, trying to make up his mind.

"Please, Curtis," I said. "I know what we're asking seems strange, but . . ."

"It would really help us out," Joe said. He looked at his watch again.

"And what do I say about Emmitt?" Curtis asked.

"Don't say anything. Leave him out of it, same as us."

Another thirty seconds or so went by before our host finally nodded. "Okay. We'll do it your way. Get out of here."

"Thanks, son. You won't regret this," Joe said, beaming. He grabbed the young man's hand to shake and nearly tore it off. I settled for a brief hug.

"Waitaminute. Where are you going with that?"

Curtis pointed at Emmitt's travel bag, which Joe had picked up and started off with.

"We'd like to go through these things again more carefully at home," Joe said. "Did I forget to mention that?"

Curtis frowned at him, not appreciating this late addendum to our deal.

"Take it," he said at last.

Joe and I ran out of the house as fast as we could manage it.

___ **5** __

On my suggestion, we ate a late lunch at the cafeteria inside the Smithsonian Institution's National Air and Space Museum. If all work and no play makes Jack a dull boy, you should see what it makes of Big Joe. I could see in his eyes that the business of trying to save Eddie's bacon was starting to weigh heavily on him, and I didn't want him losing all enthusiasm for the task on what was essentially our first day on the job. So I threw him a bone. One hour among what was arguably the most impressive collection of historic aircraft and spacecraft in the world.

He ate it up.

And, for that matter, so did I. We didn't have time to tour the museum properly, of course, but just getting to the cafeteria required one to walk half the length of the first floor, and that was an experience all in itself. For beyond the museum's main entrance—a greenhouselike web of glass and metal—prop planes and satellites, rockets and space capsules hovered overhead like mammoth butterflies, straining the cables holding them aloft as much with the gravity of their importance in aviation history as with their actual weight. Charles Lindbergh's *Spirit of St. Louis*, the Apollo 11 command module, the Wright brothers' *Flyer*— these were but a few of the dozens of authentic machines of flight the museum had on display. Even for someone like me, who had never built a model airplane in her life, it was a spectacular sight to see.

Having diverted Joe's attention from our troubles with some stimulating visuals, I now had to complete his sedation with food. The fare was nothing if not pedestrian at the museum cafeteria, but that suited Joe fine. Joe would eat in a mortician's workroom if hamburgers and fries were on the menu; his culinary tastes run from things that go well with mustard to things that go well with catsup. He ordered some kind of double-cheese heart attack on a bun and wolfed it down like a Great Dane in an Alpo commercial. All I had was a tuna salad sandwich and a bowl of mixed fruit.

While I finished up, Joe called the trailer park to check for messages. He was gone a good twenty minutes. When he returned to our table, the expression on his face was a familiar one. Joe can frown in a hundred different ways, and they all mean something different, but only one says that a Loudermilk child somewhere in the world has annoyed him. It's a look that all but shuts his right eye completely, so intense is his state of pique.

All I could do was hope it was Eddie; neither of us was strong enough to take the punishment if our haywire children were going to start ganging up on us now, sending us headaches in pairs rather than one at a time.

"What did Eddie do now?" I asked, crossing my fingers under the table.

"Who said—"

"Baby, it's all over your face. Same face I've been lookin' at now for thirty-seven years. You don't think I know when something's up?"

They can never get used to it, girls: their unfailing legibility. They let the things on their minds change the way they walk, talk, and breathe; the light behind their eyes; and the duration of their laughter—but the women they share their beds with are not supposed to notice. They think it's the devil's work, our knack for reading their emotions; I call it God-given, His way of offering us a head start when all hell is about to break loose.

"I just talked to Kozy," Joe said, using the shorthand name he had come up with as a substitute for the tongue-tying "Kostrzewski." "He just got through talking to Eddie."

"And?"

"And that fool son of ours tried to tell him he was with *us* when Emmitt was killed. We're supposed to be his alibi."

"No!"

"Yes."

"Joe, I don't believe it."

"Yeah, well, neither did Kozy, lucky for us. He talked to us first, remember? He told Eddie to lay off the fairy tales and stick to the truth, or else he walks."

I pushed my plate away. "And just what is the truth, Joe? Do we have any idea yet?"

He shook his head. "Not me."

"You think Emmitt really got killed over a book?"

"I don't know. Maybe, maybe not. But that's some coincidence, Curtis's burglar disturbing nothing but his books, if Emmitt didn't. Don't you think?"

I nodded my head. "So what now?"

"Well, we can go home to Lucille to look Emmitt's bag over again. Just in case we missed something the first time."

"Or?"

"Or we can go back and talk to the girls again."

"The girls? You mean Stacy and Eileen?"

"Yeah."

"But we just talked to them less than two hours ago."

"I know."

"Then what . . . ?"

"To ask them where we can find Vlade Divac," Joe said, pushing himself away from the table to stand up. "What else?"

"Vlade? Who's Vlade?" Eileen asked.

"We were hoping you could tell us," Big Joe said.

This time, Stacy was missing and Angus was at home. No one bothered to explain Stacy's absence, and no one asked them to try. Without discussing it, Big Joe and I must have mutually decided that two grillings in one day was a bit much to ask Eddie's friends to put up with, so we tried to keep this one brief and to the point.

"Sorry, Mr. Loudermilk, but that name doesn't ring any bells with me," Eileen said. She turned to Angus. "How about you?"

Angus shook his head too. The television in the living room was tuned to CNN and he was trying to watch it, eat a sandwich of some kind, and follow our conversation all at the same time. "Nope. Don't know any Vlades. Or Poles, in general, for that matter."

"Poles?" I asked.

"Yeah. Poles. People from Poland, or of Polish descent. That's a Polish name, Vlade, isn't it?"

"I believe it's Yugoslavian," Big Joe said.

"Vlade? No."

"I think he's right, Angus," Eileen said. "I think it is Yugoslavian."

Angus sat there and looked at us, chewing a mouthful of sandwich like a squirrel cleaning its teeth, and said, "Okay. It's Yugoslavian. I don't know any of them, either. Sorry."

"What about Curtis?" I asked. "Do you know him?"

We had told them everything about our visit to Curtis Howell's Georgetown apartment but our confiscation of Emmitt's overnight bag, afraid they might lay claim to it for some reason.

"Don't know anybody named Curtis, either. He Yugoslavian too?"

He wasn't even looking at us anymore.

Eileen was mortified. She aimed a steady glare in his direction, demanding his attention, but he refused to acknowledge it.

"Son," Joe asked him evenly, "what seems to be your problem?"

Eileen's bearded friend acted like he didn't know who Joe's question was addressed to. "Problem? Me?"

"That's right. You've had a bug up your behind ever since we came in here, and I'd like to know why."

"I think you're imagining things," Angus said.

"No, they're not," Eileen said. "You're acting like a jerk, Angus."

"Why? Because I'm not going along with their cute little Mr. and Mrs. North routine?" He directed his gaze at Joe again. "Look, I'm sorry, but this is bullshit. You think you're helping Eddie, but you're not. Eddie's in jail because he killed a man, and there's nothing you, or I, or anybody can do to change that fact. All right?"

"Here we go again," Joe said.

"Naturally, you don't believe me. You're Eddie's parents, how could you believe me? But I'm telling you the truth. Emmitt's dead, and Eddie killed him, just like he promised he would the night Emmitt died. You heard him.''

"But Eddie was here when Emmitt was killed," I said. "In bed, asleep."

"Was he? Says who? I didn't see him come in that night, and neither did anyone else. Right, Eileen?''

Eileen wouldn't answer him.

"Did you see Eddie come home that night?''

"No.''

"No. And did Stacy see him come home that night?''

Eileen's shrug was filled with remorse. "She says she didn't. No.''

"No. Of course not.''

"But what about the burglary of Emmitt's room down-stairs?" Big Joe asked. "And the break-in at Curtis's apart-ment?''

"I told you. I don't know this guy Curtis. And I doubt that Emmitt ever did either. So whatever happened over at his place is irrelevant, as far as I'm concerned.''

"Irrelevant?''

"That's right. Irrelevant. Same as your so-called 'bur-glary' of Emmitt's room. So his furniture's been rearranged a little bit. What's that supposed to prove?''

"It proves someone was down there looking for some-thing last night," I said. "That's what it proves.''

"Looking for what?''

"We told you. We don't know. But we think it was—''

"Oh, yeah, a book. I forgot.''

"Listen, son," Joe said, "we realize it sounds farfetched, but—''

"Farfetched? No. It sounds ridiculous. Emmitt was a po-litical activist, Mr. Loudermilk, not a book dealer. He barely made time in his life to read a book or two, let alone buy one.''

"You trying to tell us the man didn't own any books?''

"Of course he owned books. Back home in Flint he probably owned a small library. But out here in D.C., while he was staying here with me, I never saw him with a book in his hand once. Not once. Only reading Emmitt ever did here was in the *TV Guide*.''

"Then there would have been no books among his belongings downstairs.''

"I can't say if there were or there weren't. But it doesn't seem likely that there were, no.'' He released the sigh of an exasperated parent and said, "Look. I understand how you both feel, but this isn't getting anyone anywhere, is it? I mean, what's it going to change?''

"Obviously, not your mind,'' I said.

"Excuse me?''

"What my wife is trying to say is that you seem to have little doubt about who murdered Emmitt, and why,'' Joe said.

"You're convinced Eddie did it,'' I said. "Absolutely convinced.''

"Yes, ma'am, I am,'' Angus said, almost as if the admission were something to be proud of. "But you know something? I don't really blame Eddie. I blame myself. If I'd held my ground and allowed Emmitt to stay here when Eddie and the others were pushing me to kick him out, the trouble between him and Eddie would have never escalated to the point that it did. I'm positive of that. Making Emmitt feel like an outcast was the worst thing we could have done. It turned him into a pissed-off, vindictive asshole who wasn't going to stop leaning on Eddie until Eddie finally leaned back. Hard.''

"That's not what happened,'' I said flatly.

"Isn't it?"

"All right, all right," Joe said, interrupting the volley Angus and I had going before it could race out of control. He glared at Angus. "If you want to believe Eddie killed Emmitt, that's your prerogative. You're a grown man, and you can think what you want."

"Thank you," Angus said.

"But nobody came here to change your mind, anyway. Did we, Dottie?"

"No," I said. "We sure didn't."

"Just like you, we're entitled to our own view of things. And our view is that somebody other than our son murdered Emmitt. Now, we don't care if we ever convince you of that or not. All we care about is convincing the police. That's why we're here asking these questions. It's got nothing to do with what you think, or don't think."

"Exactly," I said.

"Now, if for one reason or another you feel disinclined to help us, you just say the word, and we won't waste another minute of your time."

"I never said I didn't want to help," Angus protested. "It's just that I don't see the point—"

"Look. You let us worry about the point, all right? You just sit back, relax, and answer our questions without all the dripping sarcasm. Otherwise, excuse yourself and let the three of us talk in peace. Okay?"

The words had been innocent, but Joe's tone was anything but; the ex-cop in my husband had just spoken, and everyone in the room understood that there was only one answer Angus could give now that wouldn't cause Joe to fall on him like a load of bricks.

"Okay," Angus said, trying to sound devil-may-care. "What do you want to know?"

"We were talking about Emmitt and books," Joe said, shifting gears on the fly.

"And I told you, he didn't have time for any. Not to buy, sell, or read."

"Yet he kept talking about buying one that was going to make him a big man in this town."

"Emmitt talked about a lot of things," Angus said.

"Then he told you about it too."

Angus started to fidget, apparently having just pointed us in a direction he had hoped we wouldn't go. "I never heard him use the word 'book.'" He paused to see if anyone would have something to say about that, then went on. "He told me it was an 'autobiography.'"

"An autobiography?" I repeated.

"Yeah. That's what he said. An autobiography."

"Whose autobiography?" Joe asked.

"I don't know. He didn't say, and I didn't ask."

Big Joe and I just looked at each other and shook our heads.

"You weren't the least bit curious?" I asked.

"What? About the details of his latest fantasy? I told you, Mrs. Loudermilk: Emmitt talked about a lot of things. And ninety-nine percent of the time, what he had to talk about wasn't real. It was just something he made up to make himself feel important."

"But how—"

"How could you tell when he was telling the truth? You couldn't. That was part of the guy's charm, I guess: never knowing when he was being straight with you, or feeding you a line of crap. He was just unpredictable that way."

"Absolutely," Eileen agreed.

"All the same," Joe said, "did this 'autobiography' story of his have any characters in it named Vlade? Or Curtis, maybe?"

"No. It didn't," Angus said.

"You're sure?"

"Yes. I'm sure."

"And you say you don't know anybody by either name yourself."

"That's right. I don't."

"What about the man who broke into Curtis's apartment? The one in the suit my wife described for you earlier?"

"Some guy with a hunk of hair coming out of the top of his head? No." Angus shook his head. "I've never seen anybody who looks like that."

"What about you, Eileen?" I asked, weary of hearing Angus's denials.

She shook her head just like Angus did, if with considerably less enthusiasm. "Sorry, Mrs. Loudermilk, but I'm with Angus. I don't know any of these people you've been asking about." When my face betrayed my disappointment, she added, "But maybe Stacy does. We can have her call you when she gets in, if you want."

"What time do you expect her in?" Joe asked.

"That's hard to say. She left without telling me where she was going." She looked to Angus. "Did she tell you?"

Angus shook his head again. It occurred to me that, in terms of what we were learning from him, there wasn't a whole lot of difference between a cooperative Angus and an uncooperative one.

We gave Eileen our phone number at the trailer park and left, before one more heartfelt "I don't know" could forever extinguish our joy in living.

___ 6 ___

Books were not in the news.

I knew this to be true, because I spent most of Wednesday night reading the *Washington Post*, frontward and backward, first page to last. I read stories about U.S. relief efforts in Rwanda; the upcoming Los Angeles murder trial of L. C. Hammond, the famous ex–football star accused of killing his estranged wife and her purported lover; the House Ethics Committee's ongoing investigation into sexual harassment charges against a Delaware senator named Graham Wildman; and an impending transit strike that was threatening to cripple the greater metropolitan D.C. area sometime the following week. I read about the suspected kidnapping of a nineteen-year-old bride who'd disappeared an hour before her wedding in Landover, Maryland; Sunday's fatal shooting of a pair of Russian tourists on the steps of the Jefferson Memorial; and an airliner crash in North Carolina that had killed thirty-seven people.

But no books.

Sure, there was one review of a historical romance novel entitled *The Feather and the Flame*, in which the reviewer took exception to the author's penchant for overusing the adjective "wickedly" ("She eyed him wickedly"; "She whispered wickedly"; "She exhaled wickedly" . . . *Exhaled*?), but that was it. As far as the *Post* was concerned, Tuesday had not been a red-letter day for the literary world.

And I can't say I was terribly surprised. By now, Big Joe and I had heard enough about Emmitt's vivid imagination to understand that what we were doing—trying to make a motive for murder out of his talk about some book he was attempting to buy—was tantamount to grasping at one very short straw. Because for all the bragging Emmitt had done, this book had no title and no subject; all anyone had been able to tell us about it so far was that it was an "autobiography" of some kind. An autobiography that was going to make Emmitt Bell a star in D.C.

Yeah, right.

It was an idea that seemed to grow more ridiculous the longer we considered it. And yet . . . *something* odd was going on relative to Emmitt. Two of his former residences had been broken into in the space of a matter of hours, and the circumstances surrounding both incidents had certainly been unusual, if not downright bizarre. In the first instance, someone had slipped into Angus's home at night, quietly but thoroughly ransacked one room—Emmitt's—and then left without ever being discovered; and in the second, in broad daylight, a man dressed like a commodities broker had forced his way into the Georgetown apartment of Emmitt's latest roommate—Curtis Howell—touched nothing but every book Curtis owned, and then taken flight when I interrupted him.

Why?

I couldn't begin to guess—but I knew that I was going to find out. I was going to find out because Eddie was counting on his father and me to prove that someone other than him could have wanted Emmitt dead—and right now, I could think of no better place to start looking for such a person than with this pair of curious break-ins, and the man—or men—who committed them.

I was hoping Stacy might be of some help in that department, but when she called us at the trailer park that evening, as Eileen had told her to, she turned out to be as full of information as Eileen and Angus had been earlier. Which is to say that I knew more about Curtis Howell and the man who had broken into his apartment than she did. And she didn't know a soul named Vlade.

Arthur Kostrzewski dropped in on us at the trailer park around eight o'clock to discuss Eddie's case. We had offered to meet him somewhere in town and buy him dinner, but he had laughed off the suggestion like someone refusing to accept a reward for helping an old lady cross the street. The man was so self-effacing and cheerful I was tempted to knee him in the groin just to see how he'd react. Would he grunt and double over, or just grin through the pain and compliment me on my technique?

He didn't need the additional inducement, but as luck would have it, Lucille made him happier still to be alive. He took one step inside her and lit up like a Christmas tree. He had never been inside a trailer home before, he said, and our Airstream's generous interior and luxurious amenities amazed him. He walked around touching the wood of her cabinetry and her kitchen fixtures like a kid set loose inside the space shuttle, eyes wide with wonder and mouth set in a grin as permanent as the Mona Lisa's. For me, it was an all too familiar sight; during our first six months on the road with Lucille, Big Joe had behaved exactly the same way.

Men and their toys. God bless 'em.

Anyway, after Kostrzewski—or Kozy, as even I had started to call him—came down from his RV-euphoric state, we all sat down at the dinette table for coffee so that Joe and I might fill him in on the highlights of our day. He praised my coffee, nodded his head at the end of our every sentence, and generally listened to what we had to say as if it were divinely inspired prophecy.

But in the end, he didn't buy a word of it.

"You don't think this angle's worth pursuing?" I asked him.

"You mean this book business?"

"Yes."

"Based upon what you've just told me? No, ma'am, I don't." He widened his smile to soften the blow.

"Why not?"

"Well, for one thing, because Eddie never said a word about it to me."

"That's because he doesn't believe it," I said.

He looked at me as if to say I'd just made his point for him.

"You don't understand," I said. "Emmitt had a repu-tation for exaggeration. So naturally, when he started telling everyone about this book he was trying to buy, no one took it seriously. Including Eddie."

"So?"

"So, just because no one believed it doesn't mean it wasn't true. Does it?"

"No, but—"

"We have to find this book, Mr. Kostrzewski. And we have to find it fast."

"You mean before this man in the blue suit you say you saw inside Mr. Howell's apartment does."

"Yes."

"I see." He nodded his head and fell strangely silent.

"Well?" I asked.

He shook his head and smiled, all at the same time. "I'm sorry, Mrs. Loudermilk, but I'm afraid I don't agree."

"Why not?"

"Because I think our time would be better spent exploring other possibilities."

"Such as?" Joe asked.

"Such as an alibi."

"An alibi?" I asked.

"Yes, ma'am. An alibi. If we could just find someone who saw Eddie at or around the time Mr. Bell was murdered, someone who could place him some distance away from the scene of the crime, we'd have a good start toward getting him off. Wouldn't you say?"

"Actually, I'd say we'd have an even better chance of getting him off if we could find Emmitt's real murderer," I said.

"Of course. But would searching for a book that may very well have been nothing more than a figment of Mr. Bell's imagination be the most efficient way to do that? I don't think so.

"You see, folks, I think the problem we're having here is that you're making too much of Mr. Bell's murder. You're operating under the assumption that it was a premeditated act, part of some mysterious and complicated plot. When in fact, the man was merely the victim of an armed robbery gone bad."

"An armed robbery?"

"Yes, ma'am. The police report states there wasn't a dime on Mr. Bell's body when they found it. No cash, no wallet, no ID. Even his pockets had been pulled inside out. Of course, the police say Eddie left him that way just to cover his tracks, but we know that isn't true. Emmitt Bell was killed and rolled that night, plain and simple. Happens to loud, argumentative drunks in dives like that every night.'' He stopped smiling long enough to sip his coffee, then said, ''Unfortunately, that doesn't mean our killer in this case is going to be easy to find. Unless he makes a mistake of some kind, that is.''

''What kind of mistake?'' I asked.

''He means letting the police find the wallet with his fingerprints on it,'' Big Joe said. ''Or using one of Emmitt's credit cards, if he had any. Something stupid like that.''

''Yes,'' Kozy agreed. ''Exactly.'' He tried his coffee again. ''I don't suppose I have to tell you what the odds are against something like that actually happening. Which is why I suggest we concentrate on finding Eddie an alibi, rather than worry about looking for Emmitt's killer. When a young man's life is on the line, expedience is everything; to make the best use of our time, we should follow the path of least resistance.

''But of course, if you'd prefer to retain someone with a different point of view, I'd certainly understand.''

He was inviting us to fire him, yet to see and hear him, you'd have thought he was asking us whether we wanted one lump or two in our tea.

''I don't think that'll be necessary,'' Joe told him. He glanced at me to make sure he'd spoken for both of us, and I just showed him a tiny shrug to indicate that he had. What else could we do?

Kozy beamed. ''Good. I'll go talk to Eddie's roommates in the morning, and then go visit the bar where Mr. Bell died. I know his friends say none of them saw him come in Tuesday morning, but it won't hurt to ask them again. Maybe someone will remember something they'd forgotten, hmm?''

He wriggled off the seat at our dinette table and got to his feet. ''Thanks so much for the coffee, Mrs. Loudermilk. It was excellent.''

''Thank you.''

He went to Lucille's door and stopped, pausing to look over her insides one more time. He couldn't have been more awed had we papered her walls with pressed gold.

''So this is a Winnebago. Simply terrific!''

He chuckled gleefully and stepped outside.

''Joe, he didn't know,'' I said, sliding over to block my husband's path to Lucille's door. There are greater crimes one can commit against a devoted Airstream owner than calling his or her trailer home a Winnebago, but there aren't many. As a matter of fact, only rape and murder come to mind.

''We've hired a moron,'' Joe fumed. ''A man who can't tell the difference between a Winnebago and an Airstream probably can't tell the difference between a hamburger and a hot dog!''

''Joe—''

''Probably sees a Lincoln on the street and says, 'Look at that swell Seville.' Or walks into a Nike store to see all the Converse shoes. Or—''

He went on like this for another forty minutes. I've learned over the years that this is how a man heals his wounded pride.

A woman cries until the hurt goes away. A man *talks* until he's too tired to hurt anymore.

And guess who gets to listen.

''Where'd you get this guy?'' Eddie asked. It was Thursday morning, back at the District of Columbia Jail.

"Who?"

"Ko-stof-ski, or Ke-zew-ski—whatever his name is. My lawyer. Mr. K."

"The proper pronunciation of his name is 'Koz-ref-ski,' but we just call him 'Kozy,' " I said.

"What you ought to call 'im is 'Happy the Clown.' Man acts like he never had a bad day in his life."

"Eddie—"

Beside me, Big Joe started chuckling, unable to do anything else. I tried to take the high ground and remain stoic, but that lasted all of sixty seconds. Even Eddie had to laugh after a while.

It was good to see he still knew how.

We told him all about our busy day Wednesday, and asked him if he could help us make sense of any of it.

"I don't think so," he said.

"You don't know anyone named Curtis Howell?" Joe asked him.

"No."

"Or Vlade?"

"Vlade like the basketball player?"

"Yes. V-L-A-D-E, Vlade."

Eddie shook his head. "No." He paused. "I know a guy people *call* Vlade, but I don't think that's his real name. It's just what people call him."

"Who is this?" I asked, sitting up in my chair.

"Boy we play ball with out at the park. Down at Meridian Hill."

"You're talking about basketball," Joe said.

"Yessir. Basketball."

"What do you know about this boy?"

"What do I know about him? He's got a good outside

shot, and he likes to go to his left. Besides that, not much.''

"You don't know his real name?"

Eddie shook his head. "Uh-uh. 'Less his real name is Vlade. That's all I've ever heard anybody call him, 'Vlade.'''

"Why would they call him Vlade if that wasn't his real name?" I asked. It was a question I'd kept expecting Joe to ask, but it didn't look like he was ever going to feel the need.

"Because he looks like Vlade Divac," Eddie said. "What else?"

"How do you mean?"

"I mean he's a tall, dark-haired white boy who wears a beard. And he looks kind of foreign. Middle Eastern, or something, just like Vlade Divac."

"Did Emmitt know him?" Joe asked.

"Vlade? Yeah, he knew 'im. Emmitt used to play up at Meridian, same as me. We even went together, a couple of times."

"How did they get along?"

"How did they get along?" Eddie thought about it before shrugging his shoulders. "They got along okay, I guess. Same as they did with everybody else, anyway."

"But no better or no worse than that."

"Huh?"

"Your father wants to know if they were *friends*, Eddie," I said.

"Friends?"

"Yes," Joe said. "Friends. As opposed to two guys who could take each other's company or leave it. Did they just play ball together, or did they hang out?"

"I don't know about them hangin' out," Eddie said, "but . . . now that you mention it . . ." He let the thought merely dissipate, as his face slowly grew dim.

"What?" I asked him.

"I don't know. I was just thinking that they *did* kind of laugh and joke a lot between games, now that I think about it. And Vlade . . ." He stopped again, not sure if he should say what was on his mind or not.

"What about him?"

"He's a little crazy. Intense. On the court, anyway."

"You're saying he's prone to violence," Joe said.

"I'm sayin' I've seen him go off on people, yeah. More than a couple of times."

"You think he could have killed Emmitt?"

Eddie produced another shrug. "I don't know. If he got mad enough, he could have, yeah. But it's hard to say for sure, right?"

It wasn't the definitive answer Joe had been hoping for, but it was either press Eddie all day on the subject, or move on. So we moved on.

"You wouldn't happen to know where this 'Vlade' lives, would you?" Joe asked.

Eddie shook his head emphatically. "Dad, I just told you—the boy's a headcase. A wild man. You think I'm gonna tell you two junior-G-men where to find 'im?"

"You want out of here, don't you?"

"Yeah, but—"

"Nothing's going to happen to us, Eddie," I said. "We'll be very careful, I promise."

Eddie considered us in silence for a moment, trying to stand firm. But then his eyes started wandering about the room we were in, with its drab gray walls and bar-lined windows, and he remembered something he'd apparently forgotten, if only for a moment: He *did* want out of this place, and now. At any cost.

"I know somebody who might know where he lives," he said.

"Who?"

"Another homeboy who plays up at Meridian named Ahmed. Him and Vlade are tight, I know because they used to ride to the park together in Ahmed's car."

"Wonderful," I said. "So how do we find Ahmed?"

"He sells souvenir T-shirts on the Mall. Down by the Washington Monument. I see him down there all the time—he's probably there right now."

"The mall? What mall is this?"

"You know, the Mall. That big, long park that runs between the Capitol Building and the Lincoln Memorial. With all the jogging paths and reflecting pools. That's called the Mall."

"Oh."

"Ahmed works down there?" Joe asked.

"Yessir. His table's right next to the Washington Monument, like I said. Down near the northeast corner of the block."

"What's he look like?"

"He's a real thin brother. Dark-skinned, medium height. He looks like a starving Ethiopian, he's so thin. The guys up at Meridian mess with him about it all the time. But . . ."

Joe and I turned to each other and exchanged nods.

"Look," Eddie said. "Near as I can tell, Ahmed is cool, but I still don't like the idea of you guys goin' down there to hassle him about Vlade. You ask me, if somebody's got to go talk to 'im, it should be Mr. K. That's what you guys are payin' him for, right?"

"Mr. K. has his own agenda to follow," I said. "And we don't want to bother him with ours. Besides, I already told you, we're going to be careful. If Ahmed acts like he doesn't want to talk to us, that'll be the end of the discussion. Your father and I will just walk away."

Eddie looked at Joe, who raised an eyebrow and rolled his eyes, an obvious commentary on the value of the promise I'd just made. I made a mental note to crown my husband later.

"We're going to be okay," I told Eddie.

"You'd better be. I've got enough worries in here, I don't need to be worryin' about you guys, too."

He tried to smile, but there was nothing behind it but pain. Two days in jail, going on three, and he already had the broken heart of a man serving a life sentence with no possibility of parole.

"Don't worry, baby," I said. "You're going to be out of here real soon."

It was another hollow promise, of course, but it sounded good to say it, just the same.

____ 7 ____

We had been on the mall once already and hadn't known it.

It's the rectangular, three-and-a-half-mile-long hub of the city, a huge green concourse surrounded on all sides by many of D.C.'s most renowned museums and monuments, the Smithsonian's aviation museum we had visited the day before among them. The giant, white-domed Capitol Building lies to the east, the hallowed halls of the Lincoln Memorial to the west, each fronted by a crystal-blue reflecting pool of dissimilar shape and size. To the north, the National Gallery of Art and the Smithsonian's museums of natural and American history share Madison Drive with the east wing of the U.S. Court House; to the south, the Botanical Gardens building and the D.C. War Memorial play end pieces to seven more Smithsonian museums, including the aviation museum, the Freer and Sackler galleries, and the Smithsonian Castle. Each and every edifice on the Mall has an architectural character all its own, from the multiple glass domes of the Botanical Gardens to the red brick totality of the old Smithsonian Castle, and each is intriguing in its own way. But nothing draws your attention faster or holds it longer than the Washington Monument. Nothing.

Though in truth the Capitol Building stands taller, its right to the highest point in the land actually protected by law, the Washington Monument appears to tower above it and everything else, like a giant among Lilliputians. A white, four-sided needle of marble and stone, it commands the center of the Mall in relative isolation, climbing from its base at the top of a gently sloping hill to a height of 555 feet. Approached from any angle, it looks like the inverted finger of God driven into the earth.

Big Joe and I stood among the halo of pennants ringing the Monument's base for a good thirty minutes before we started looking for Ahmed. The Mall is comprised of roughly eight city blocks, and at the four corners of each of the centermost six, street vendors sell everything from hot dogs and lemonade to souvenir postcards, baseball caps, and guidebooks. And T-shirts. Hundreds and hundreds of T-shirts. Table after table is lined with them, cotton billboards emblazoned with myriad designs touting some facet of D.C. They come in every size and every color, and as bargains go, they are a steal.

In fact, they practically sell themselves, which was a fortunate thing for Ahmed, as his idea of hawking them was to sit in a lawn chair behind his table and wait for someone to hand him some money. There was a striped awning over his table that cast a generous shadow over him, and he couldn't have looked more cool and content if he'd been sitting in a wading pool filled with ice and Corona beer. He had a spot right off the northeast corner of the block, just as Eddie had said, and he looked exactly the way our son had said he would, like a dark-skinned poster boy for famine relief. Even sitting in his chair, wearing a plain white tank top over bright orange Bermuda shorts, he looked painfully fragile.

"How're you folks doing?" he asked us when we stepped up to his table. A toothless smile was all he could muster in the way of hearty salesmanship.

"Fine," Joe said. "We're looking for Ahmed."

"I'm Ahmed." He didn't seem to be afraid to admit it. "Somebody recommended me to you, huh?"

"You might say that."

"In that case, you get a special price. Ordinarily, the shirts are five bucks each, or three for twelve dollars. But for you, I'll let you have five for fifteen, today only. Not bad, huh?"

"Actually, we didn't come here for T-shirts."

"You want sweatshirts? I usually sell 'em for ten bucks apiece. For you they're eight each, or two for fifteen. Best deal in town."

"We wanted to talk to you about Vlade," I said, cutting to the chase.

Joe gave me a sideways glance, but didn't say anything. I assumed that meant either I'd done okay, or he was too ticked off to scold me without going completely ballistic.

"Vlade?" Ahmed said the name as if it were foreign to him. "Who's he?"

"We understand he's a friend of yours," Joe said, forcing his way back into the conversation. "Someone you play basketball with at . . ." He looked at me. "What was the name of that park?"

"Meridian," I said.

"Meridian Hill? Hey, I play with a lot of cats up there," Ahmed said. He had yet to so much as stir in his chair or raise his voice above a level of sheer indifference.

"We're told you drive this one to the park on occasion," Joe said.

Finally, the T-shirt salesman betrayed a note of actual interest in what we were saying by falling silent. Then he went beyond that and demonstrated something akin to concern by getting to his feet. "Okay, folks," he said calmly. "What's this all about?"

"We've got a son in jail for a murder he didn't commit, and we think your friend Vlade can help us get him out."

"Who's this? This son of yours, I mean."

"His name is Eddie Loudermilk. He's played with you up at Meridian too, he says."

Ahmed nodded. "Yeah, that's right. I know Eddie. All offense, no defense." He laughed at his little joke. "So who'd he kill, anyway?"

"He didn't kill anybody. I told you. He's been falsely accused of killing an ex-roommate of his, a boy named Emmitt Bell."

Ahmed shook his head. "Never heard of him."

"Eddie says he used to play with you too."

"Maybe he did. I don't learn everybody's name who plays up there. Only the ones who have game."

"Game?" I asked, not following him.

"Yeah, you know. Moves. Hops. A money shot."

"He means talent," Joe said.

"Yeah, exactly. Talent. If this brother you're talkin' about—what was his name?"

"Emmitt."

"If Emmitt didn't have any, I didn't know him. I didn't know him 'cause I didn't *wanna* know him."

"But Vlade did. That's why we want to talk to him."

"You think Vlade killed him?"

"No. I didn't say that. We just want to talk to him, that's all."

"If you could tell us where he lives—" I said, before Ahmed started shaking his head to cut me short.

"Sorry, people, but I can't do that. I give you homeboy's address, next thing I know, *he'll* be gettin' busted for somethin' *he* didn't do."

"We wouldn't let that happen," Joe said.

"Maybe not. But if it *did* . . ." He shook his head again. "I can't do that to my boy. I'm sorry."

"Maybe if you told him we have his book," I said, without having the foggiest notion why.

For the second time in five minutes, Big Joe turned his gaze on me, only this time his motives were not in question. He was ordering me to shut up—just as the captain of the *Titanic* must have instructed his crew to watch out for icebergs *after* the infamous ocean liner had struck the granddaddy of them all.

"What book?" Ahmed asked. He was curious, but perhaps nothing more than that; it was difficult to say for sure.

"He's been looking for a book, and we have it," I said. "If he'll give us ten minutes of his time, we'll give him his book. It's as simple as that."

"I don't get it," Ahmed said.

"No, but Vlade will," Joe said. "And that's what's important, isn't it?"

Ahmed had to think about that one.

"Tell us where we can find him, Ahmed. Otherwise, the wife and I are gonna give up. Give his damn book to the cops, and let them track him down. It's your call, son."

Ahmed studied our faces for a long time, looking for a reason to believe we were bluffing. We just stood there and turned his gaze right back on him, a united front he wasn't going to dent, no matter how long he chose to try.

"You got a pen?" he asked us eventually.

I fished one out of my purse and handed it to him. He

wrote an address down on the back of a business card and
gave it to Joe.

"This is his place here," he said. "You go over there
right now, you might catch him before he leaves for work.
Otherwise, you're gonna have to wait till after six, when
he gets off."

"We'll go right now," I said. "Thank you."

"Look. Just do me a favor and don't tell him how you
found him, all right? I got enough enemies in this world, I
don't need another one."

"We won't tell him a thing," Joe said.

"And if you really are thinkin' he killed this cat Emmitt,
you're way off base. Homeboy works with paper, not guns
and knives. He wouldn't know what to do with either one,
believe me."

"We'll see," Joe said.

And then we left to do just that.

The address Ahmed had given us led us to a four-story
brick apartment building on Fourteenth Street Northwest,
just north of Logan Circle and less than a mile west of
Howard University. Half of its windows were barred with
sheets of plywood, and the other half held only meager
shards of glass. Its walls were pockmarked with graffiti,
and garbage was piled in heaps on the sidewalk out front,
waiting for sanitation trucks that were never going to come.
I'd never been here before, of course, and there were no
signs out front to identify it, but I knew what this was all
the same, and so did Joe.

"Jeez, Dottie, this is a crack house!" he said.

It hadn't exactly come as a total surprise. To get here,
we'd had to drive through a nightmarish neighborhood that
promised little else. Nothing we had seen of Washington,
D.C., to this point had seemed to justify the city's reputa-

tion as one of the most crime-ridden in the country, but we understood now that our view of D.C. as a whole had been woefully incomplete. Away from the power and glamour of the city's celebrated core, pockets of heart-rending poverty like this one loomed, where all the usual outcasts of the American Dream—i.e., destitute men and women of color—were encamped. One minute, Joe and I had been riding past a magnificent Gothic-style cathedral, and the next, a burned-out shell of a gas station surrounded by the skeletal remains of a dozen stripped-down cars and trucks. It had been like passing through a door between heaven and hell.

The impulse to turn tail and run was a strong one, naturally, but neither Joe nor I succumbed to it. We had some discussion about it, but we didn't succumb to it.

"You're right. It does look like a crack house," I said, getting out of our truck and closing the door behind me. *"Dottie!"*

Joe opened his door and stood up on the running board, glaring at me over the Ford's roof. A handful of black teenagers were perched on the apartment building's stoop, watching us intently. "Where do you think you're going?"

"I'm going inside. Aren't you?"

"No. And neither are you."

"Joe, we can't argue about this out here on the street, now. We're attracting too much attention as it is."

Joe screwed his face up into a mask of husbandly frustration and said, "Please don't make me get out of this truck and tackle you, woman. I'm askin' you nicely."

"Joe, we have to go in there. And we have to hurry." I looked at my watch; it was almost eleven o'clock. "If we don't catch Vlade at home before he leaves, we'll have to wait all day to try him again, like Ahmed said. And we don't want to have to come back out here after dark, do we?''

His answer was the one infallible sign a man gives a woman when she's won an argument by technical knock-out: silence. Women can surrender in a million different ways, but men only know to shut up.

"Lock the truck up and come on, baby," I said. I threw in the "baby" just to make it easier for him to forgive me later.

Being a mature adult over fifty doesn't have many advantages, but one of the few it does have is the calming effect we sometimes have on the young. Much is said about how little young people respect their elders these days, but I've found that most teenagers still reserve their best behavior for those occasions when older people like Joe and me are present. I don't know why. Where a younger couple trying to ease past the quartet of boys milling about the front stoop might have been subjected to any number of physical atrocities and humiliations, Joe and I managed it relatively unscathed. We received a few hard looks, and had to endure several crude, mumbled words of curiosity, but other than that, no one bothered us. Perhaps the expression on Joe's face, and the breadth of muscle straining the buttons on his shirt, had something to do with this, or maybe we were just lucky. Either way, we got inside the building easily enough.

Not that the view improved in there. In fact, it only got worse. The hallways were pitch-dark and lined with walls shedding paint in huge sheets, and there were holes in the ceiling you could drop a forklift through. The floors were damp here and there and the overall aroma of the place was an overpowering combination of urine, mildew, and rat droppings.

"I don't know about this, Dottie," Joe said.

I shrugged. "I don't know about it either, but we're here now. Let's just go to the boy's room and get it over with."

He nodded his head and led the way up a staircase of dubious reliability to the second floor, where the sound of a crying baby was deafening. We were looking for apartment 28. We came to learn it was the last door on the right, directly opposite what our ears told us was the source of all the crying, apartment 27. We still hadn't seen a soul inside the building, but that could have been because we weren't looking very hard.

Before I could take the initiative and knock on the door, Big Joe pushed his way past me to do it himself. I didn't stop him.

"Go on in," someone suddenly standing behind us said.

I knew it was Ahmed before I even turned around. His voice carried the same air of unwavering indifference it had back at the Mall. The gun in his hand *was* a surprise, though.

"Door's not locked," he said. "And the man's expectin' you."

Big Joe and I just stood there and regarded him for a moment, reviewing our options. Then we realized we didn't have any.

"One of us saw this coming," Joe said to me, "and it wasn't you."

"Later, later," I said, trying to hush him. Then, to Ahmed, I said, "How did you get here so fast?"

He shrugged and smiled, showing us the few remaining teeth in his mouth. He really needn't have bothered. "I knew where I was goin'. You didn't. Makes a big difference in this city." He gestured smoothly with the gun. "Come on, let's go. I'm in a hurry."

Joe opened the door as instructed and the three of us stepped inside the apartment. It was a shambles, of course, just like the rest of the building, but it wasn't empty: As promised, Vlade was waiting for us there. Or at least someone who fit Eddie's description of Vlade. He was a tall, dark white man with a full beard and a beak for a nose, with a head full of curly black hair and eyes that peered out of two shadowy sockets like the headlights of a train emerging from a tunnel. I figured him to be six four or six five, using Joe's six two as a yardstick, and at least 220 pounds. I won't tell you who I used for a yardstick there.

Ahmed closed the door behind us and said, "This is them," intending the comment for his friend. He looked uncomfortable with the gun in his hand, but not necessarily unskilled in its use.

"Don't know 'em," Vlade said. He had the unsettling baritone of a perpetually angry man. He stepped forward for a better look, like someone examining two used cars for sale, and asked, "Who are you?"

"Are you Vlade?" I asked.

He turned to Ahmed and said, "She does that again, answers a goddamn question with a question, shoot her. Him, too."

Ahmed nodded wordlessly.

"Now . . ."

"We're Eddie Loudermilk's parents," Joe said, before Vlade—if he *was* Vlade—could repeat the question. I don't know how he did it, but there wasn't a trace of fear or anxiety in my husband's voice.

"Eddie who?"

"Eddie Loudermilk. You play basketball with him at Meridian Hill Park sometimes."

"So?"

"So you also knew a friend of his. Emmitt Bell. He used to play ball with you too."

"Your son knew Emmitt?"

"They were roommates once, yes."

"Where?"

"In a town house out in Dupont Circle. But you probably already know that, unless . . ."

"Unless what?"

"Unless somebody else broke into Emmitt's old room there two nights ago, and not you."

Joe waited for him to deny it.

"Why would I want to do something like that?"

"To look for a book," Joe said.

Vlade and Ahmed exchanged a lingering glance, a silent acknowledgment that they were nearing the Promised Land. "What do you know about my book?" Vlade demanded.

"Then it *is* your book."

"Yeah, it's mine. I asked you what you know about it."

"Not much. Other than that's probably what got Emmitt killed."

"You haven't read it?"

"No. Did you murder Emmitt?"

The question stopped Vlade cold. "That's answering a question with a question again, old man," he said.

Joe didn't say anything, and looked as if he wouldn't for some time. The old devil had ice water in his veins.

"No. I didn't kill him," Vlade said, capitulating.

"But you know who did."

"We weren't talking about Emmitt. We were talking about my book."

"What about it?"

"Ahmed says you have it."

I was afraid that subject was going to come up, sooner or later.

"Not exactly," Joe said.

Vlade's eyes narrowed and anger stretched his mouth into a harsh horizontal line. We hadn't noticed it before, but he had been closing in on us as we spoke, so that now he was less than an arm's length away from either one of us.

"What do you mean, 'not exactly'?" he asked.

"I mean that we don't have it in our possession, but we know where it is," Joe said.

"So where is it?"

Big Joe shook his head. "I'm afraid that's all we can tell you for now, son."

"Say what?"

"I said, you want the book, and we want our son out of jail. You have a problem, and we have a problem. That's why we're here. Now, we don't give a damn about your book, and you don't give a damn about our son, but if we can find a way to cooperate with each other, we can all go home happy. Otherwise . . ."

Vlade threw a hand up to silence him, seething. "I don't have time for this, old man," he said.

"Then stop playin' Mr. Tough Guy, and let's cut a deal."

"Man, fuck this," Ahmed said, speaking for only the second time since we'd entered the room. "They don't wanna talk, let's just do 'em and get outta here. I gotta get back to work."

"Shut up," Vlade said.

"Excuse me?"

"I said shut the fuck up!" He held the other man's gaze until he was sure no retort was coming, then turned his attention to Joe again. "What's your problem, old man? You crazy or something?"

"I'm not crazy. And neither is she. We just know better than to give you what you want before you've answered the questions we came here to ask."

"Maybe I'll get what I want no matter what you do. You ever think of that?"

"Maybe you will."

"I could have my boy Ahmed here put a bullet in your old lady right now. Think you'd want to talk to me then?"

"I think if you touch either one of us, you and Ahmed are in for a long night. That's what I think."

I didn't realize my mouth was hanging open until my jaw began to hurt. I was the one who had come up with this silly "We've got the book" bluff in the first place, so I was hardly in any position to complain, but what Joe was doing now was tantamount to building a three-bedroom extension onto a backyard toolshed. The meager foundation of my lie just wasn't going to hold up.

Or was it?

"I don't care what you say, old man," Vlade said. "You *are* crazy." Then: "I'll give you five minutes. Then I want my goddamn book."

"Whoa, whoa, whoa," Ahmed cut in. "Hold up a minute, Taz, man. You're not *buyin'* this crap?"

Taz?

"I'm not buying anything 'cept a little insurance," Vlade—or Taz—said, apparently having missed how Ahmed had just referred to him. He only looked at Joe again, a glimmer of newfound respect in his eyes. "Man says I'd be better off doin' things his way, and I believe him. We'd get him to talk eventually, sure, but we'd probably have hell doin' it. He's a pain in the ass." He glanced at me. "Her, too."

"You'd better believe it," I said. Feeling brave.

"I don't believe this," Ahmed said.

Vlade's eyes never left Joe's. "Well?"

My husband didn't waste any time getting to the important stuff. "If you didn't kill Emmitt, who did?"

Vlade shrugged. "I don't know. I wasn't there when it happened."

"You mean at the Zoo Room?" That was the name of the bar where Emmitt had been killed. "You weren't there the night Emmitt was murdered?"

"I was there, yeah. But I didn't see it happen. It happened out in the alley while I was still inside. Waiting."

"Waiting for what?"

"For the little punk to come out of the men's room. What else?"

"You were there watching him?"

"Yeah. I didn't think he'd spotted me, but I guess he did. They were throwin' a sheet over his body by the time I went into the john and found the open window he'd crawled out of."

"Then you never saw him with a man in a blue suit," I said, taking a shot in the dark.

"A man in a blue suit?"

"That's right. Almost bald, but not quite. Has this clump of hair growing out of his head like this," I said, using my right hand to show him where the odd-looking fountain of hair had sprouted from the scalp of Curtis Howell's burglar.

"Oh, yeah, yeah, yeah. You mean the cop," Vlade said, nodding.

"The cop?"

"Yeah, the cop. What did you think he was, a barber?"

"We thought he was a government man of some kind."

"A government man? You mean a Fed?"

All I could think to do was shrug.

"A Fed, a cop—same difference," Vlade said.

"Then he *was* there that night?" Joe asked.

"He was there, sure. He a friend of yours or something?"

"No. Just somebody we've seen around before, that's all," I said.

"Yeah? Like where?"

"Like in Curtis Howell's apartment," Joe said. "He broke in there yesterday, looking for your book."

"Who's Curtis Howell?"

"Just a friend of Emmitt's he'd been staying with when he died. You didn't know him?"

"No."

"But you knew his phone number."

Vlade appeared nonplussed. "Did I?"

"You called Emmitt over at his place at least once that we know of. Curtis was the one who answered the phone."

Vlade shrugged again. "Okay. So I knew the man's number. So sue me."

Joe paused, possibly taking a moment to decide that time spent discussing Curtis Howell was time poorly spent. "Let's get back to this cop," he eventually said.

"What about him?"

"He's no friend of ours, but maybe he's a friend of yours. Is that possible?"

"It's possible, sure. But I don't know the man."

"Then how is it you remember him so vividly?"

"I remember he was there. That's all I remember. I told you, I was there to watch Emmitt, not him."

"And you were there watching Emmitt because . . ."

"Because I wanted my book back, man. What the hell do you think?"

"How did he get it in the first place, if it belonged to you?"

"He stole it. How else would he get it?"

"He didn't *buy* it?"

"Buy it? Hell, no. He couldn't come up with the cash to buy it, so he did the next best thing. He broke into my apartment and ripped it off." He had to smile at the audacity—or shortsightedness—of the man. "I guess he didn't think I'd be able to find him again. But I did."

"At the Zoo Room."

"Yeah. At the Zoo Room. Your boy Eddie led me right to him." He was grinning.

"Eddie?"

"That's right. I figured one of Emmitt's friends would have to hook up with him, sooner or later, so I started watching the house where they were all staying. And sure enough, that night, Eddie goes out to the Zoo Room and puts Emmitt on his ass." He laughed at the memory.

"You saw that?" Joe asked him. "You saw them arguing?"

"Sure. So what?"

"Then you must have seen Eddie leave afterward, too," I said, following my husband's lead.

"Yeah, I saw him leave. Is that all you wanted to hear?"

"Not all, no, but—"

"Look, to hell with this," Ahmed said angrily, finally piping up again. "Your five minutes are up. Tell the man where his book is, or I'll kill you both. I'm tired of listenin' to this shit."

Joe and I looked to Vlade for help, but all the white man did was shrug. He'd given us our five minutes, just as Ahmed had said, and now it was time for us to pay off.

But with what?

"Where's my book?" Vlade asked.

Joe and I looked at each other, no doubt praying that one of us would resemble someone who'd just had a great idea. But all we saw on our respective faces was an almost comical mask of shattered hope and desperation. It was the same doomed look the Coyote always had on his face just before another Road Runner trick flattened him like a pan-cake.

Joe reached out for my hand, and I took it.

"We don't have the slightest idea," Joe said to Vlade.

I closed my eyes and waited for Ahmed's gun to go off.

When the explosion came, it was louder than I had ex-pected. It sounded more like a cannon being fired than a pistol. And the concussion that went with it—an unantici-pated side effect—nearly knocked me off my feet. All this from a little black handgun? I wondered.

"Hold it right there! Police!" someone behind me shouted.

I opened my eyes.

A young black policeman in a dark blue assault uniform was standing in the apartment's open doorway, training a handgun of his own on the room. He had a baseball cap on his head and a flak jacket over his chest, and yellow sten-ciling on both clearly identified him as an employee of the "MPD," lest someone mistake him for a plumber armed for bear. We had the view of him we did because he'd kicked the apartment door down, which explained the loud bang and rush of air I'd heard and felt only moments be-fore. It also explained why Ahmed was stretched out on the floor, unconscious, having apparently had the misfor-tune of catching the displaced door with the back of his head when it came crashing off its hinges.

As a second policeman similarly attired appeared from the hallway to join the first, Big Joe and I raised our hands over our heads and waited for further instructions. But Vlade . . .

. . . was *gone*.

We turned around to look for him and found ourselves looking at an open window and the fire escape beyond. Even from where we were standing, we could hear the big man racing down the metal stairs to the street. The black cop went to the window to give chase, but by the time he got there, Vlade was just a memory, and a distant one at that.

That left only Joe and me to explain the gun in Ahmed's hand.

We did the best we could.

8

So Joe's initial sense of the place had been correct.

It *was* a crack house.

As it happened, neither Ahmed nor Vlade really lived there, but several drug dealers did, and the District of Columbia Metropolitan Police Department knew it. What they didn't know was that someone had tipped the dealers off to their impending raid, which was why the apartment they had found us in—and much of the rest of the building—was all but empty upon their arrival. Poor Ahmed had chosen the site for our meeting with Vlade thinking it was the perfect place to grill us, then kill us in relative peace, and only twenty-four hours before, it might have been precisely that. But on this Thursday afternoon, it was ground zero, the ideal spot for the authorities to come crashing down on him like a toppled skyscraper. In other words, the man's timing had been lousy.

Of course, the same could have been said about mine

and Joe's, as the police eagerly reminded us time and time again. Once they were satisfied we were telling the truth about who we were and what our motives were for being where they'd found us, they couldn't tell us enough how lucky we were to be alive. First the vice squad officers at the scene gave us a piece of their minds, then their superiors downtown, and finally, two familiar faces named Dobbs and Early—the homicide detectives in charge of Eddie's case.

Joe and I had been answering questions up on the second floor of an M.P.D. building on Indiana Avenue for almost two hours when Dobbs and Early appeared, acting like they'd both been dragged from a sound sleep to be here. We were sitting alone in the interrogation room, catching our breath and comparing notes, when the pair walked in, each wearing a scowl that would have looked right at home on a totem pole.

It almost made us sorry that we'd sent Kozy home. We'd called him in to counsel us during our interrogation session with M.P.D. vice squad people, but once we figured out he was there just to smile, we decided we could do without. So we sent him home, under protest. It was no great loss.

Anyway, Dobbs and Early quickly reintroduced themselves, then went right to work making us feel like ants who had crashed the wrong picnic.

"How would you two like to spend the weekend in jail?" Dobbs asked, crossing her arms in front of her chest the way Joe likes to do when he's angry. She was a tall blonde in a dark gray suit and white silk blouse, as severely attractive as a woman who never smiled could be, and she was standing over us like a kindergarten teacher about to dispense with two troublemakers.

"Jail?" Joe said.

"That's right. Jail. Would you like that?"

"You can't put us in jail," I said, without an ounce of conviction.

"I beg to differ with you, Mrs. Loudermilk, but we most certainly can," Detective Early said. He was sitting in a corner near the door, on a chair turned backward to face his heavy frame. His suit was gray too, but he'd either just rolled down a hill in it or never gotten around to ever having it pressed. "You and your husband disrupted a police operation that was nine months in the making. The boys in Vice are out for blood. Now, you say it was just a coincidence, your being there, but they're not so sure. They think maybe you were there for the specific purpose of getting in their way, to prevent them from making any arrests. People like you have been hired to do that sort of thing before."

"That's ridiculous," Big Joe said.

"Is it?" Dobbs asked. "We don't think so. It's certainly no more ridiculous than *your* explanation for your presence there."

"Ridiculous or not, what we've told you is the truth," I said. "Ask Ahmed, he'll tell you."

"We have. He says he saw you two entering the building alone and went in after you to see if you were lost or something. He said he didn't want to see you get hurt in there."

"Give me a break. The man was holding a gun on us!" Joe said.

"He says you pulled the gun on *him* when he tried to help you," Early said.

"That's nothing but a load of bull, and you know it."

"All the same, it's the story he's telling," Dobbs said, "and as you may have noticed, it does nothing to corroborate yours. Does it?"

Joe didn't answer that, and neither did I.

"Bottom line here, Mr. and Mrs. Loudermilk, is that Detective Dobbs and I are all that's keeping you from spending the next couple of nights in the slammer," Early said. "Our friends in Vice want you locked up, like I said, but if we lean on 'em hard enough, we can probably get 'em to cut you some slack. The question is, what happens if we do? You gonna go back to your hotel and leave the police work to us, or are you gonna keep runnin' all over town lookin' for ways to get yourselves killed?"

"We aren't interested in getting killed, Detective," I said. "We're only interested in getting our son out of jail."

"Seems to me that should be his lawyer's job, not yours," Dobbs said.

"Is there a law that says we can't help him?"

"If your idea of helping him is disrupting an ongoing homicide investigation—yes, ma'am, there is."

" 'Ongoing' investigation?" Joe asked. "What ongoing investigation?"

"Just because we have a suspect formally charged and in custody, Mr. Loudermilk, doesn't mean we aren't still working the case," Early said.

"If you're still working the case, why are *we* the ones out looking for Vlade's book?" I asked him.

"Because there is no book," Dobbs said.

"How do you know that?"

"Because unlike you, Mrs. Loudermilk, Bud and I are professionals at this sort of thing, and we know a false lead when we hear one. 'A biography that was going to make Emmitt Bell a big man in this town.' Really."

"We didn't make this up, Detective. We were told about the book. By several people."

"You mean you were told about a book Bell claimed to have."

"Yes. What—"

"What's the difference? I'd say quite a bit. It's like the

difference between seeing an alien yourself, and hearing someone talk about the time *they* did.''

"What about Vlade?" Joe asked. "He was prepared to kill us for the book. It sure as hell wasn't imaginary to him."

"Ah yes, Vlade. The bearded mystery man you say leapt out a window before anyone but you could get a good look at him."

"He *did*," Joe said, rapidly losing his cool.

Dobbs let out a big, theatrical sigh. "Okay. He did. You want us to talk to him, you tell us how to find him. With nothing but a first name and a physical description to go on."

"Providing Vlade really is his first name," Early added.

"Would it be any easier if his first name were Taz, instead?" I asked, only now recalling how Ahmed had dropped that name at the crack house.

"Taz? Now his name is Taz?" Dobbs asked.

I told them where the name had come from, and Joe backed me up, ostensibly remembering the incident now that I'd mentioned it.

Dobbs turned to her partner. "You know anybody named Taz?"

"No," Early said, a little too quickly for my liking. Something about his bland expression had changed, but I couldn't put my finger on what it was.

Dobbs looked at me again. "Sorry, but I don't know any Tazes, either. Or Vlades, for that matter."

"You could always look those names up on the department's computer," Joe said.

"If we had any reason to think it'd be worth the trouble, we could do that, yes. But we don't. Not at this time, anyway."

"Not at this time?"

"That's what I said."

"In other words, there's a possibility you could change your minds later."

"No, in other words, we've got better things to do with our time. But if our own investigation into your son's case somehow led us to believe this Vlade/Taz person was worth talking to—"

"He knows why Emmitt was killed, and you don't think he's worth talking to?" I asked, my own temperature rising fast.

"Please, Mrs. Loudermilk. Not the 'government man' at the Zoo Room again," Early said. (Even though Vlade had referred to the man in the blue suit as a cop, we'd continued to call him a government man around Early and Dobbs, for reasons that should be obvious.)

"But Vlade said he was there that night!"

" 'A government man.' A *government* man! Do you have any idea how worthless that description is in this town? They're *all* government men out there, Mrs. Loudermilk! Describing someone as a government man in Washington, D.C., is like referring to a runner in the Boston Marathon as 'the guy wearing Nikes'!"

"But—"

"As I was saying," Dobbs said, cutting me off, "if our own investigation should lead us to believe *any* of the people you've mentioned here today—including this 'government man' of yours—are worth finding and talking to, we'll certainly make every effort to locate them. All right?"

"Your *own* investigation," Joe repeated.

"Yes. Our own," Dobbs said.

"The one that's still ongoing."

Dobbs glowered at him, not caring for his dig in the least. "That's right."

"And where does this investigation take you now, I won-der?"

"I'm afraid we're not at liberty to discuss that, Mr. Loudermilk," Early said, before his partner could answer.

"But it's safe to say neither Vlade nor Ahmed figure into it. Is that right?"

"Ahmed will be held overnight, of course," Early said. "Vice can hold him that long just for being in that building when they came in. But unless you two choose to charge him with assault, or we can find a way to pin a possession charge of some kind on him, that's it. After tonight, he walks."

"In that case, we want to file charges," I said.

The two police detectives glanced briefly at each other; then Dobbs said, "If that's what you want to do, fine. You're certainly free to do so. But I should warn you, the chances of getting a conviction are pretty slim. Without witnesses—"

"My wife said we want to press charges," Joe said, is-suing what was clearly the final word on the subject.

"Like I said, that's fine," Dobbs said, shrugging. "Our only concern is that you stay out of our way from here on in. Bud and I will pull you out of the fire this time, but that's it. We can't do our job and babysit you two, too. I'm sorry."

"What the lady's trying to tell you is, we catch you sticking your noses into our investigation again, we're go-ing to lock you up for a while," Early said. "For your own protection, of course."

Dobbs stared us down. "Do we make ourselves clear?"

This time, it was Joe's and my turn to exchange a quick glance. The message I read in his eyes was the same one I was hoping he'd read in mine: *We'd better say what these people want to hear.*

First Joe nodded his head, then I nodded mine, and neither of us felt the least bit guilty about telling such a huge and transparent lie.

Who feels guilty telling lies in Washington, D.C.?

"Joe, what are we doing here?" I asked.

We were back at the trailer park inside Lucille, well into a second straight hour of drinking coffee and watching TV. To see us, you'd have thought all that had happened over the last seventy-two hours had happened to two other people, and not us.

"It's called laying low," Joe said, flipping through the pages of the *TV Guide*.

"Do we have time for that?"

"No. But we're gonna *make* time." He got up from his chair to refill his cup, working hard to avoid my gaze.

"Joe—"

"Listen. We're gonna hang out here for a while and wait for things to calm down a little. Because Ahmed may be out of our hair for the moment, but his pal Vlade's not. He's still out there somewhere, remember?"

And he thinks we have his book, I thought. It wasn't that I'd forgotten Vlade, it was just that I preferred to pretend he didn't exist, because it was too frightening to do otherwise. He *was* still out there somewhere, as Joe pointed out, and though he probably had no idea where to find us, I could imagine him looking for us all the same, determined to exact some kind of revenge on the two fiftyish smartasses who had dangled his book in front of his nose and then run out on him before delivering it. In a city the size of D.C., Joe and I could probably go about our business exactly as we had been for the last two days and never run into him again, but in the unlikely event we *did* . . . well, of such chance meetings are double funerals made.

Still, hiding out in the reassuring confines of Lucille struck me as a coward's way out, especially when you considered that Eddie was counting on us to be a little more creative with our time.

"Joe, we can't sit here forever," I said.

"Forever, no. But we should sit tight here for the rest of the day, at least."

"And do what? Eddie—"

"Eddie's fine, Dottie. Okay? Stop worrying about the boy so."

"Joe, he's in *jail*."

"I understand that. But I think your concern is misplaced. If there's anyone you should be worried about, it's the poor bastard he's sharin' his cell with, not Eddie. By now, that man's had to listen to our son's antiestablishment mumbo jumbo for two whole days, and if he hasn't tried to hang himself with a pillowcase yet, it's for sure he'll try tomorrow." He laughed.

I gave him a look designed to fall just short of icy.

"Okay, so maybe that wasn't funny," he said, returning to his chair with a fresh cup of coffee for each of us. "But I still say you're worrying too much. In or out of jail, Eddie can take care of himself. If it were Bad Dog or Walter in there, I'd say you might have reason to be concerned, but Eddie? No. Not Eddie. Eddie's gonna be just fine."

After giving the matter some thought, I had to admit he had a point. More than any of our other children, Eddie was a survivor; no matter what he came up against, he had always managed to come out on top, and generally without a scratch.

"I guess you're right," I said, sampling my coffee.

"Of course I'm right." He reached over to pat my knee. "But like I said—we're not giving up. We're still gonna get him out of there. We're just gonna wait till tomorrow morning to start in again, that's all. To give Vlade some time to forget how we lied to him today, number one, and to give our friends Dobbs and Early the warm and fuzzies, number two.''

''The warm and fuzzies?''

''Yeah, you know—a good feeling about things. Unless I miss my guess, they're gonna be watching us for a while. But if we can give them the impression all that huffing and puffing they did this afternoon scared us off—sent us running here to hide—they just might lose interest in us and go away. That's a long shot, I know, but it's worth a try, right?''

''I suppose so,'' I said. ''It's just . . .''

''What?''

''It's just that I can't shake the feeling we're wasting precious time, just sitting around like this. There's half a day left out there; we should be doing something constructive with it.''

''Something constructive?''

''Yes.''

''May I make a suggestion?'' He put his coffee cup down and turned his body in his chair to better face me.

''Joe, don't even think about it,'' I said. I tell you, if it weren't for bad timing, men wouldn't have a sex drive at all.

''What?''

''I said keep your pants on.''

He frowned as if wounded. ''I was going to say, if you want something constructive to do, you could try going through Emmitt's bag again.''

I studied his face for clues to his sincerity, then said, ''Uh-huh.''

He started laughing.

I went to the bedroom to retrieve the bag and brought it

back to my chair. I had to squeeze past Joe in the kitchen area on my return, as he was now standing in the aisle there, paying careful attention to something pinned to the corkboard we keep on the wall.

"And stay away from that calendar," I said when I'd taken my seat again. This time, I was the one laughing.

In the last year, he had gotten in the habit of making these tiny little drawings on the calendar, marking certain dates in the past that were generally about four or five weeks apart. The dates meant nothing to me, and neither did the drawings. Initially, they looked like little firecrackers going off, but lately they'd changed to hearts. I made him change to hearts the day I finally remembered to ask him what the firecrackers were meant to commemorate, because I hadn't been able to figure that out on my own. It should have come to me when I saw how he reacted to the question—like he had no idea what I was talking about—but it didn't. I had to hear it from him to finally understand.

The firecrackers meant "bang."

"Bang?" I had asked.

He nodded his head, twisting his mouth in an odd shape in order to keep himself from grinning.

"There was a 'bang' on those dates?" I asked, still as dumb as an ox. And then, of course, I thought about what I'd just said, and all became clear to me.

He was using the calendar to document our lovemaking schedule. Because at our age, he said, it's sometimes difficult to tell whether it's been forty-two days since you last did something, or forty-two years, and he wanted to make sure that when it *felt* like he needed it, he really did need it. He didn't want to burn me out asking for more than he was due, he said.

I chased that man all over the trailer park that day. (And later that night, looked over his shoulder as he drew the first of several cute little hearts on our calendar.)

"Now, wait just a minute," Big Joe said today, still examining the calendar despite my order to desist. "This ain't right."

"I told you to get away from there," I said.

"This is not the way I draw a heart. No way."

"Joe—"

"And I don't remember us doin' anything on the twenty-fifth. The twenty-fifth was just two weeks ago!"

"Joe, you're imagining things." I was laughing again, though I didn't really want to.

He stood there in the kitchen and glared at me, hands on hips. He wasn't laughing himself, but you could tell he wasn't too far from it. "Woman, I catch you movin' hearts up on this calendar, I'm gonna file papers on you the next morning," he said.

I unzipped Emmitt's overnight bag and began to empty it, pretending I was too preoccupied to hear what my husband was saying.

Nothing about the contents of the bag had changed. As before, all I found were eight pair of boxer shorts, four colored T-shirts, five pair of socks, two pair of denim pants, a toothbrush, deodorant, a small vial of cologne, some dandruff shampoo, and one plastic bottle of mouthwash. Two of the T-shirts had pockets, but they were just as empty as the pockets of the pants. The bag itself had three pockets— one on the side, and one on each end—but they, too, were empty. I turned the bag inside out, and removed the cloth-covered sheet of cardboard lining its bottom. Nothing. I even held the clear plastic bottle of mouthwash up to the light to see if anything was floating around inside it—but nothing was.

"No luck, huh?" Joe asked.

"No. If there's a book here, it must be smaller than the

naked eye can see." I put everything back inside the bag and zipped it closed again.

"You checked everything?"

"Yes. You sat right there and watched me, didn't you?"

He nodded his head. The television was still on, but only because neither of us had thought to turn it off. On late weekday afternoons like this one, there wasn't much to see on the tube but talk show after talk show, hosted by people who were often more bizarre and intriguing than the guests they were interviewing. In this corner, you had Sally and four women in love with the same Elvis impersonator; in that corner, Montel and his teenage children of cross-dressing moms. Gone were the days when the only non-sense on daytime television was supplied by harmless soap operas. Now, the medium's pap came in the form of endless chatter between gay policemen and the chiefs who had fired them. Or dwarfs and their unfaithful spouses. Or . . .

And to think nobody in America wanted to read any-more.

I looked up at the set to catch the tail end of an info-mercial of some sort. For steak knives or cassette tapes, a home gym or a garden tool—something like that. An an-nouncer was telling me where to send my check or money order for $39.95, reading the address displayed on the screen out loud in case I was sightless and beginning to feel left out of the action. He read it three times. "P.O. Box blah-blah-blah, Somecity, Somestate, Zip-zip-zip. Again, that's P.O. Box blah-blah-blah, Somecity, Somestate . . ."

I was about to get up to turn the set off myself when the idea hit me.

Emmitt's bag had an address tag on it. Just a little leather sheath tethered to the handle, holding a small white card behind a clear plastic window. Emmitt's name and a Mich-igan address were written on the front of the card. I reached into the slit on the back of the tag and pulled the card out, then turned it over to inspect the other side.

And there was the book.

Or at least the title and author of one. "Get It in Writing—The Power of Modern Litigation by Charles S. Bermann and Susan Hale." It was written in the same handwriting as that on the front of the card.

"Joe, take a look at this," I said, my voice betraying my excitement.

Looking away from the TV, Joe took the card and examined it. "This came off the bag?"

"Yes." I gave him a moment to look the card over, then said, "That's the book we've been looking for, isn't it?"

He nodded, his eyes still on the card. "If it isn't, somebody's playing games with us," he said.

"But that doesn't sound like a biography."

"*The Power of Modern Litigation*? No. It doesn't. It sounds like a lawbook of some kind. But I guess we won't know for sure what it is until we read it, will we?"

"Trouble is, we still don't know where it is."

"True. But at least now we know what we're looking for, and that's a start." He finally looked up from the address tag to face me again. "So much for layin' low, huh?"

We were out the door inside of a minute.

"Never heard of it," Angus said.

"*Get It in* what?" Stacy asked.

"*The Power of Modern Litigation*?" Eileen repeated.

Joe and I felt pretty smart that we'd called them first before driving out to see them. It would have been a wasted trip. They knew nothing about the book, and didn't recognize the names of its authors.

"That's supposed to be the book that was going to make Emmitt famous?" Eileen asked.

"I don't know if it is or not," I said. "But he wrote this down on the back of the address tag on his overnight bag for some reason, don't you think?"

"But that sounds like a law school text or something."

"Maybe that's what it is."

We had our choice of many, as one might expect, but we ended up visiting the one in the heart of downtown Alexandria, less than four miles from the trailer park. Home to some of the D.C. area's most beautiful and history-rich attractions, including the boyhood home of Robert E. Lee and the George Washington National Memorial, Alexandria was a virtual wonderland of eighteenth-century Americana. Only a time machine could do more to make one feel a part of our great nation's Colonial infancy.

Unfortunately, like everything else in Washington we'd managed to steal a taste of so far, this was a sensation Joe and I were able to experience only briefly, rather than savor. It was nearly four o'clock, and the Alexandria library was due to close at five. We parked the truck quickly and rushed inside.

"Explain to me again why we're here," I said. "Suppose we find a copy of the book in here. What good does that do us? It's only the copy Emmitt had, or was trying to buy, that we should be interested in, isn't it?"

"Probably. But not necessarily. How will we know until we learn more about the book than its title and the names of the people who wrote it?"

He'd made his point.

We found one of those computer terminals that all libraries have now in lieu of a card catalog and ran a search for the book we were looking for, but it didn't turn up. We searched by title, both authors together, and each author individually, and the results were the same each time. The closest we came to a match of any kind was a book entitled

Given to Exaggeration by Suzanne Hale; a close cousin to Susan, perhaps, but the wrong S. Hale nonetheless.

The librarian stationed at the reference desk—a tall, rakish brunette who told us her name was Lorraine—explained that the book's absence from the computer's database only meant that it was not part of the District of Columbia Library's collection, and should not be taken as an indication that the book did not exist. She showed us to the reference section and a set of volumes there called *Books in Print*, about thirty large, hardbound books which were divided into three categories: Subject, Title, and Author.

"We'll try searching by title first," she said, pulling the *G* volume of the Title subset from the shelf. But *Get It in Writing* wasn't there.

"We'll try authors next," she said.

On page 81 of the *B* volume, she hit pay dirt.

"Here it is," she said, handing the book over to me.

With Joe close at my side, pressing in to get a good look at the book on his own, I read the following: "Charles S. Bermann & Susan Hale. *The Power of Modern Litigation*. 344p. 1964. 22.95 (0-32155-12-1) Hollins & Sons."

"What happened to *Get It in Writing*?" I asked, more than anything just thinking out loud.

"I don't know," Lorraine said.

"This doesn't really tell us much," Joe said, and I didn't argue with him.

"What were you hoping it might tell you?"

"Well, we hoped it might more clearly define what *kind* of book it is, for one thing," Joe said. "I mean, it's a lawbook of some kind, obviously, but is it a college text, a professional reference manual, a coffee table book—what?"

The librarian reached out, asking for a second look at the volume in my hands. "May I?" I handed it over and watched as she studied the entry again. "It certainly doesn't sound like a coffee table book," she said.

"That tells us a little more about the book than we already knew, but not much," Joe said. "We now know who published it, and when. Unless I'm missing something."

"Other than page count and Library of Congress number, no, you're right. That's all that's here," Lorraine said.

"Would you expect it to say more if, say, the book was valuable?" Joe asked.

"Valuable? How do you mean?"

"I mean rare. A collector's item. Like a five-hundred-thousand-dollar first edition or something."

Lorraine nodded her head, catching on. "I follow what you mean. No, there'd be no mention of anything like that here. These entries simply don't go into that kind of detail, as you can see."

"Then how—" I started to ask.

"How can you find out if the book is valuable? Come with me, I'll show you."

She put the volume of *Books in Print* back where she found it, then led Joe and me over to another row of reference books. As she scanned the shelves, something made me turn and look behind us. A brief flash of movement at the corner of my eye, or a small sound that somehow didn't belong in this quiet place; I don't know what it was. But something made me turn—

—to find nothing there.

A man and two women, all young, sitting at a table reading. A mother and son walking away. A tired and disheveled-looking man sitting in a chair by himself, poring over a stack of magazines resting in his lap.

Like I said: nothing.

Joe caught me staring and asked, "What is it?"

I shook my head. "I don't know. I guess nothing."

"Vlade?"

"No. But I'll bet that's what it is. He's got me spooked.
I'm imagining things." I smiled to reassure him.

"Here we are," Lorraine said.

We turned in time to see her pull something off the shelf
entitled *American Book Prices Current*. It was about the
size and weight of a good dictionary.

"If there's anything rare or valuable about the book
you're looking for, you should find it listed in here," she
said, handing the book over to Joe. "This is the most com-
prehensive and up-to-date listing of collectible books we
have."

Big Joe cracked the book open and started flipping
through its pages. I just stood back and let him look, deciding I didn't have the energy to stand on my tippytoes
and squint over his left shoulder in an effort to peruse the
book with him. I found out soon enough it would have been
pointless to do so in any case.

"Looks like it isn't here," Joe said, clearly disappointed.

"No?" Lorraine asked. "Did you look under both *The
Power of Modern Litigation* and *Get It in Writing*?"

"Yes. Neither title is here." Joe returned the book to
her. "Can you think of anything else that might help us?"

"I'm sorry, no. At least, nothing immediately comes to
mind. But maybe if you came back tomorrow . . ."

"Sure." Joe shook her hand. "Thanks very much for
your time."

"Yes, thank you," I echoed.

"I'm sorry I couldn't help you more," the librarian said.
"I just wish . . ."

She was working her way up to asking a question,
though neither Joe nor I actually needed to hear it; her face
was already posing it. "You want to know what our interest
is in the book," Joe said.

"If you wouldn't mind telling me," she said.

Joe looked at me and shrugged, putting the onus on me to decide. To Lorraine, I said, "Without going into all the ugly details, we have a son in some serious trouble with the law, and we think this book could get him out of it somehow. Only we don't know anything about it except what we just read. Which isn't much of anything, as you've seen for yourself."

"I see." She was nodding her head thoughtfully, as if she really did see. "Is it one particular copy of the book you need, or would any copy do? Do you know?"

"We don't know," I said. "But we'd settle for any copy we could find."

"Of course." She paused, thinking. "What about the publisher? I'm sure if you called or wrote them, they'd be able to round up a copy for you somewhere."

"If time weren't a consideration, that would be a good idea," Joe said. "Unfortunately, every minute counts."

Lorraine nodded her head again, watching her left foot tap the floor absently. "You only need to *read* this book, correct? That is, you don't need to actually *possess* a copy?"

Joe looked at me to see if I knew how to answer that, but I only shrugged at him. "That's hard to say," he said. "I *suppose* all we need to do is read it, but—"

"*Joe!*" I screamed, cutting him off abruptly.

This time when I'd turned around, I'd seen him: standing at the edge of a distant aisle, peeking around the corner of one of the book stacks to steal glances at the three of us. Mr. Blue Suit with the Funny Haircut, last seen running for the exits like a weasel caught in the henhouse.

"It's him! The government man!"

His suit was brown today instead of blue, but that was the only thing different about him I could see. Even his way of saying hello was the same: The minute he saw me pointing at him, he took off for the door, moving like a man trying to outrun a bullet.

Something at my right shoulder blew past me and I had a sneaking suspicion it wasn't Lorraine the librarian. It was SuperJoe, ageless manhunter. Most women have to worry about their husbands chasing after *women* half their age, but me, I've got a husband who likes to run down the *men* in that category. His intentions are different, of course, but the risks to his health are the same. Not that he ever actually *catches* anybody anymore; he just takes up pursuit and continues it until his legs cramp up or his lungs give out, whichever comes first.

And here he was at it again.

Naturally, I had to take off after him, if only to identify the body when he collapsed in the street. I'd moved pretty quickly, but he was almost a full block away by the time I made it out of the library and onto the sidewalk.

"Joe! He might have a gun!"

He either didn't hear me, or heard me and chose not to listen. You'd think after all these years, I'd be able to tell the difference, but I can't. At least, not from a distance. Joe just kept going, the white man in the brown suit setting the pace for him nearly twenty yards ahead. They were both pushing past pedestrians and crossing streets against the light, bouncing off people and cars like flies off a screen door. Once, Joe stumbled and went to a knee, but before I could reach him he was gone again, huffing and puffing anew.

After three blocks of this, the white man scurried left around a corner and disappeared from view. By that time, he'd managed to open up a one-and-a-half-block lead on Joe, and I'd managed to close within three or four yards of my husband. Joe turned the corner less than two minutes later, and I was right behind him—but we were both too late. Joe had already stopped running when I reached him, reduced to a mere observer as our quarry raced past us in the opposite direction, sitting behind the wheel of a white sedan that had burned considerable rubber peeling away from the curb.

"Damn!" Joe said, bending over to catch his breath. He didn't look too good.

"Are you okay?" I asked, bending over to wheeze right along with him.

"I'm fine," he said.

"I don't have to tell you how dumb that was. Do I?"

"No, but I bet that's not gonna stop you from tellin' me anyway."

"He could have killed you." I paused to take a few deep breaths. "If he had had a gun—"

"He would have used it four blocks back. Before it became obvious to him he was putting the length of a football field between us every sixteen seconds."

Despite the circumstances, I got a kick out of that. He did too. Getting old's no picnic, but it's only unbearable if you never try to find the humor in it.

"So what now, Jesse?" I asked him, knowing he'd get the joke. Track-and-field great Jesse Owens was one of Joe's all-time favorite athletes.

"We call Mo and find out who that was."

"How would she know?"

Joe grinned at me. "By making a few phone calls, I imagine."

I had to study his grin for another long moment before I understood. "You got his license number."

"George-Nancy-five-one-five-two," Joe said proudly.

"Way to go, baby. Care to race me back to the library?"

I may never have said anything less amusing in my life.

9

Mo said we'd have to wait until the next morning for her to get us the information we needed. We tried to think of a way to make our request sound innocent, so she wouldn't have to know what the license number meant or how it had come to our attention, but it just couldn't be done. We knew the less we told her, the more she'd demand to know, so we just told her the truth up front and finished with an order that she hold all the usual objections for some other time, some other place.

The last didn't do us a bit of good.

She nagged and fussed, ranted and raved. What were we doing running after strangers in the street, why weren't we staying at the trailer park and letting Eddie's lawyer handle things, didn't the police tell us to keep our noses out of their investigation, blah-blah-blah . . . First I had to hear it, then it was Joe's turn. That child kept us on the phone for fifteen minutes, listening to all her warnings and reprimands—and she was just getting started. After fifteen minutes, she *really* got down and dirty.

She threatened to cut off our money supply.

And she could do it too. The way Joe and I have our finances set up, Mo controls everything. *Everything.* If a bill needs paying, Mo has to pay it. Trailer camp reservations, insurance premiums, stock transactions, income tax filings—you name it, Mo handles it. Without her, the Joe and Dottie Loudermilk traveling circus would have to fold up its tent and go home—providing we had enough gas money between us to get there.

It was a terrifying thought, improbable or not.

"Mo, don't even play like that," I told her.

"Who's playing? You and Daddy have to be stopped, Mother. Your adventures get more outrageous every day. Evel Knievel never tried this hard to kill himself."

She wasn't going to cut off our money and she knew it, but just planting the idea in our minds was her way of saying she was genuinely afraid for us, and was growing weary of constantly being asked to play reluctant accomplice to our self-destruction. Sometimes it's actually a blast to watch a grown child suffer the same kind of exasperation over your behavior that he or she routinely put you through in their youth (or, in the case of Joe's and my children, perhaps only a week ago last Tuesday), but it isn't always. Sometimes you feel for the child, and find yourself wishing they could learn to love you, and worry about you, just a little bit less than they do. That's how it is with us and Mo. Her concern for us is often overbearing and annoying, but it's always real and deeply heartfelt. Joe and I are a very significant part of her everyday life, and she has no problem demonstrating that she wants to keep it that way for as long as the good Lord sees fit to have us all around.

This is why, no matter how irritating her grumbling becomes, we always let her speak her piece before saying our good-byes. And whether she lets us have it for five minutes or fifty, there is one thing she never fails to do: threaten to jump on a plane and come babysit us. It's usually the first thing she says, but not this time.

I knew afterward there'd been something funny about our conversation, but not until Joe and I were in bed that night did I figure out what it was.

"So?" my husband said. Famous last words.

Nine-thirty the next morning, I answer a knock on Lucille's door, and who do you suppose I find standing outside, suitcase in hand?

"Little girl, I don't believe you," I said, shaking my head.

"It's good to see you, too, Mother," Mo said, wearing a mock frown.

She moved to kiss me and I surprised her by pulling her to me and kissing her first. Physical intimacy has always been difficult for Mo, so our hug was as brief and awkward as usual, but I enjoyed it even if she didn't.

"Something told me you were going to do this," I said, taking the bag from her hand and pushing her inside Lucille ahead of me. She hadn't taken two steps through the door when Joe was on top of her, swallowing her up in his arms like a balloon he was trying to pop. Joe has a soft spot in his heart for all of our kids, but the spot he reserves for Mo is about the size of a small island. It always has been, and always will be. There's a connection between those two that borders on the unnatural.

"Turtle!" he cried, laughing. "What a surprise!"

A surprise, he says. I tried to tell him the night before she might pull something like this, and he didn't want to believe me.

"Daddy, I thought I told you what you can do with your

'Turtle,' " Mo said, pushing away from her father playfully.

"Look—I've been calling you Turtle since you were three weeks old, and I'm not gonna stop now. So you may as well just get used to it."

Joe had given her the nickname because, as an infant, she had spent so much time on her back, like a turtle that had flipped over and could not get up. I never learned to use the name much myself, but that was just as well, because Mo might have taken her own life by her fifteenth birthday if I had. I mean, a turtle isn't exactly the first thing that comes to a young girl's mind when she's searching for a positive self-image, now is it?

"Before you two get too carried away, just let me say that after the three of us have some breakfast and talk, your father and I are taking you right back to the airport," I said to Mo, only half joking.

"Oh no we're not," Joe said.

"Joe, she's mothering us. I didn't ask this girl to come out here, and neither did you. We can handle things here just fine by ourselves."

"I am not mothering you, Mother," Mo said. "I'm simply offering you the benefit of my assistance."

"No you're not. You're meddling. And if we let you get away with it this time, you'll do it again. We can't have you dropping in on us like this every time you think we're in trouble, Mo. We can't, and we won't."

"Now, Dottie—" Joe said.

"And you be quiet! I'm trying to send the girl back home, and you're treating her like a rich uncle!"

That made Joe chuckle, and pretty soon we were all laughing.

Later, as the three of us sat at the dinette table finishing up the breakfast I'd promised, we asked Mo about the license plate number we'd asked her to check on for us the day before.

"Well, actually, that's really why I'm here," she said, her expression turning grim.

"What is it?" Joe asked.

"That number you gave me's a government plate all right. It belongs to one of the cars in the congressional motor pool. I tried to find out who, specifically, that particular car's assigned to, but I couldn't. They don't make that kind of information available to the general public, for obvious reasons."

"The congressional motor pool?" Joe said.

"Then that means the man we were chasing yesterday is a U.S. congressman?" I asked.

"Or someone on one of their staffs, yes," Mo said. "An aide or a Secret Service man. Someone like that. That's why I thought I'd better fly out here. If you two are messing with people like that, you're going to need all the help you can get."

I shook my head. "I don't understand," I said.

"Neither do I. So maybe we ought to go over this whole thing one more time. From the beginning."

And that's just what we did. Starting with our drive up to Angus's home from the trailer park Monday evening, to our phone call to Mo less than eighteen hours earlier, Joe and I recounted everything that had happened to us over the last four days, including every detail we could remember. Mo asked questions, we answered them, and when we were done . . .

. . . we *still* didn't know what in the world was going on.

"So we still don't have a copy of this book," Mo said.

I shook my head. "No. We checked back with Eddie's friends early yesterday evening, about an hour after we talked to you, and they said the book wasn't there. The same goes for Curtis Howell. He looked for it in his apartment, but couldn't find it there, either.''

''What was it called again?''

''*Get It in Writing—The Power of Modern Litigation.* Here, I'll show you the card.'' I went to my purse and came back with the address card I'd taken off Emmitt's bag.

After examining the card for several seconds, sipping a glass of juice as she did so, Mo said, ''I think I've read this book. Back when I was in school.''

''You have?''

''Yes. But I don't remember this first part of the title— *Get It in Writing*. The book was just called *The Power of Modern Litigation*, by these two authors. It was a textbook, I think.''

''Funny you should say that,'' Joe said. ''Because the listing for the book we saw at the library was under that title too. *The Power of Modern Litigation.* There was no mention of *Get It in Writing*.'' He looked at me. ''Was there?''

''No,'' I said. ''We even asked the librarian about it, we asked her why they would drop the first part of the title like that, and she said she didn't know.''

Mo was studying the address card again. ''Have either of you spoken to Art this morning?''

''Art? Oh—you mean Kozy?''

''Kozy?''

''That's what we call Mr. Kostrzewski. Kozy.''

''Very cute. Have either of you spoken to 'Kozy' this morning?''

''Not yet. Why?''

''I don't know. I just had an idea I'd like to run by him. Where can I find a phone?''

''There's a pay phone out by the manager's office,'' Joe

said, standing up. "Come on, I'll show you."

They were only gone about ten minutes. I'd barely finished clearing the dishes off the dinette table when they climbed back into Lucille again, both of them acting like the trip had been more than worthwhile.

"Well?" I asked.

"Well, he doesn't have the book either," Mo said, beaming. "But he did solve one mystery for us." She paused for effect. "I didn't think 'Get It in Writing' was part of the book's title, and I was right. Art says Get It in Writing is the name of a *book store* here in D.C. A used-book store out near George Washington U."

"A book store?"

"Yep."

"And how much do you wanna bet they've got at least one copy of *The Power of Modern Litigation* on the shelf somewhere?" Joe asked.

"You called them?" I asked.

"No. We're just going to drive out there and look for ourselves. Kozy had an address for the place and everything."

Mo was still grinning from ear to ear, extremely proud of herself. "Well? You coming along or not?"

It was a tough decision to make. Go with my husband and daughter, or stay behind and wash the dishes.

I really hated to leave those dishes too.

Get It in Writing was a large, two-story storefront along the hub of Washington Circle in Foggy Bottom, a mixed-bag section of D.C. bordered by the Potomac River, Constitution Avenue, and Seventeenth and N streets. Only blocks from George Washington University, it was a hushed and nearly deserted temple to the god of the written word, its interior spaces jammed to the rafters with used books. Everywhere you looked, a tidal wave of book spines threatened to crash down upon you.

It didn't seem possible that any form of order could be at work here, but it was. Before we could approach him ourselves, we watched a middle-aged black man wearing a "Get It in Writing" T-shirt field another customer's question at the desk, show the customer to a distant aisle, and then hand him the book he was looking for. Just like that, straight to the source, without any hesitation whatsoever.

"Can I help you folks?" he asked when he returned to the desk. He had more gray hairs in his beard than he had good teeth in his mouth, but that didn't stop him from trying to grin Mo right out of her shoes.

"We're lookin' for a book called *The Power of Modern Litigation*," Joe said, trying to force his way into the forefront of the man's attention. "By . . ." He consulted Emmitt's address card. "Charles S. Bermann and Susan Hale."

"The Power of Modern Litigation," the man repeated, his eyes still focused on Mo. "I guess that would be a lawbook of some kind."

"Yes," Mo said, rewarding him with a smile of her own.

"Let's go take a look," he said.

He took us up a creaking wooden staircase to the second-floor loft. The lighting there was weak, and the air thick with dust, but neither condition deterred our guide in the least. In fact, he went about his business as if nothing short of Armageddon could ever prevent him from finding a book, once he had the scent. Without appearing to so much as glance at the signs labeling the stacks, he walked straight to the center of an aisle, looked up to his right, and pulled down a medium-sized hardcover book from the first shelf from the top, handing it to Mo like it was Volume One of the Dead Sea Scrolls.

"Here you are," he said, beaming. I've seen people present Academy Awards with less pomp and circumstance.

Feeling neglected, Joe stepped forward and took the book from Mo's hand before she could open it. He looked her toothless friend dead in the eye and said, "Thank you." Dismissing him. It was a little unkind, but necessary; the bookseller's infatuation with our daughter was such that he might never have left us alone without being invited to. In retaliation, he made his departure a painfully slow thing to watch.

"Okay, he's gone," I said finally, moving in to get a closer look at the book in my husband's hands. Mo did likewise on his other side.

There wasn't much to the book jacket, just black block letters on an alternating background of red and blue: "The Power of Modern Litigation by Charles S. Bermann and Susan Hale." A subtitle read: "Finding the Keys to Success in Today's Complex Legal Theater."

"This is it," Joe said, whispering conspiratorially.

And then he opened the book.

We all had the same thought immediately after, but it was Mo who actually verbalized it.

"Wait a minute," she said.

The pages were all handwritten, some in blue ink, some in black, and beautifully so. Times and dates were recorded at the top of most, and the headings of some of these even included a specific locale. The Capitol Hill; the Le Mistral; 601 Pennsylvania; the Dirksen.

"Jeez Looweez," Joe said, still whispering.

It was a diary, written in one of those leatherbound blank books sold in stationery stores. The book jacket it wore was just a disguise, no doubt taken from a similar-sized copy of *The Power of Modern Litigation* residing elsewhere in the store.

"It's a diary," Mo said.

"A diary?" I asked, bewildered. We were all whispering now, even though we still seemed to have the second-floor loft completely to ourselves.

"Yes. Isn't that what it looks like to you?"

"Of course it's a diary," Joe said. "Angus said Emmitt was tryin' to buy an autobiography, remember? And that's what a diary is, isn't it? An autobiography?"

Before anyone else could suggest it, he started flipping back through the book to its first few pages, hoping to come upon a title page of some kind, but all there was in the way of that was one blank page marred by a single inscription at its center: "VOL 8."

"Damn. No title page," Joe said.

"But the author's name has to be in there *somewhere*," I said, starting to feel a bit overwhelmed by all the twists and turns this ride to save our son was putting Joe and me through.

"Let me see that again, Dad," Mo said. As she examined the book once more, taking what felt like an eternity to turn its pages, Joe and I watched her face for clues to what she was thinking, and neither of us liked what we saw. What seemed at first to be grave concentration soon took on the look of fear—and Mo wasn't big on fear. The kinds of things that frightened Mo usually brought most other people to their knees.

"What is it, Mo?" I asked nervously, glancing over my shoulder for what must have been the tenth time in the last five seconds.

"These names," she said. "Dave Hewitt, Cal Alexander, Betsy Richardson, Jimmy Benson . . ."

"U.S. senators?" Joe asked.

Mo nodded. "I see at least a dozen names I recognize

here, maybe more.'' She fell silent again, reading on. ''It's unbelievable.''

''What?''

She didn't answer him.

''Mo, your father asked you—'' I started to say.

''This is all one big kiss-and-tell book, that's what. The author's misadventures with this woman or that woman, and the member or members of Congress who sometimes went along for the ride.'' She finally looked up from the book to face us again, looking like a television news anchor with nothing but bad news to report.

''Wait a minute. You don't mean—''

She nodded her head. ''Yes, Mom, I do. I could be wrong, but I think this diary belongs to Graham Wildman.''

''Jeez Looweez,'' Joe said.

And I'd never heard that said at a more appropriate moment.

10

We had one of Graham Wildman's diaries. Or something that sure looked like one, anyway.

Wildman was the senator from Delaware who for the last several months had been facing a House Ethics Committee investigation into charges he had sexually harassed several present and former members of his female staff. At one point during the Committee hearings, while testifying in his own defense, the fifty-seven-year-old senator had inadvertently revealed the existence of a set of diaries he kept which supposedly outlined, among other things, the everyday details of his sex life, and the Committee had been demanding it be granted access to those diaries ever since. Wildman's response to that demand, as one might expect, had been short and to the point—"I'll see you in court"— and that was where things stood today, in the limbo between what the Committee wanted and what Wildman was willing to surrender.

After taking the diary downstairs and paying less than four dollars for it, without ever letting on to Mo's infatuated friend that what we were buying was not, as its phony cover continued to suggest, a copy of *The Power of Modern Litigation*, Mo, Big Joe, and I rushed back to our truck and just sat in the cab for a while, to discuss what our new discovery meant and what, exactly, we should do with it.

"Well, this certainly explains a few things," Mo said, sitting between her father and me on the truck's bench seat. "Like how this little adventure of yours could possibly involve people who drive around in congressional motor pool cars, for one thing. And why Emmitt thought that book would make him a big man in this town, for another. God, I'll bet there isn't a man, woman, or child on Capitol Hill who wouldn't give their right arm just to read its first five pages. If Emmitt had wanted to sell it, he could have named his price. Between the tabloids and Wildman's enemies alone, he would've had potential buyers coming at him from all directions."

"Absolutely," Joe said.

"In fact, I'll bet that's exactly what happened. Only—"

"Only one of those potential buyers figured it might be cheaper to kill him and look for the book later than to pay him off."

"Yes. If he'd been blackmailing Wildman, for instance—"

"Waitaminute, waitaminute," I broke in. "I think you two are forgetting something, aren't you? This was supposed to be Vlade's book, remember?" I raised the diary in my lap to show them its bogus cover again, as if that might refresh their memories. "If there was a small fortune to be made by selling it, or by using it to blackmail Wildman, why in the world would Vlade have been willing to let Emmitt have it for a paltry five hundred dollars?"

"That's simple," Joe said. "Because he didn't know what it was."

"Excuse me? He didn't know what it was?"

"That's right. He knew he had something worth sellin', yes, but he didn't know its true value. So he underpriced it. People make that kind of mistake all the time."

"Joe, all the man had to do was read—"

"Who said he could read? Did we ever see him read?"

"No, but—"

"But what? Maybe the man can't read, Dottie. And if he can't read, he can't know what the book's really worth. Can he?"

Well, he had me there. Just because Vlade owned a book didn't mean he knew how to read it. It was unlikely that he couldn't, but in this age of rampant illiteracy, anything was possible.

"All right. So maybe he can't read. I'm not convinced that's the answer, frankly, but for now, let's just say it is. How did someone like that get his hands on a Graham Wildman diary in the first place? Through the Book-of-the-Month Club?"

"How does any lowlife get anything? Obviously, he must have stolen it," my husband said.

"Stolen it? Joe, you can't be serious. Senator Wildman's been trying to protect those diaries of his for three months now; he's probably buried them so deep in the ground you couldn't dig one up with a bulldozer." I turned to my daughter. "Don't you think, Mo?"

She took a long time to shrug. "I guess."

"You guess?"

"What I mean is, I understand what you're saying, Mom, and you make a good point. Stealing one of Wildman's diaries should have been next to impossible, for this Vlade character or anyone, as well hidden as Wildman probably had them. But the fact remains, he got hold of one somehow. And I don't think the good Senator gave it to him as a Christmas gift. Do you?''

It was a question that required no answer, but my silence gave it one anyway.

"Of course," Mo said, "there is one other possibility we've yet to consider."

She glanced quickly at the book in my lap, offering me a clue.

"The diary's a fake," I said.

Mo nodded. "Why not? Just because it reads like one of Graham Wildman's diaries doesn't mean it has to be one."

"A fake?" Joe said. "This?" He took the book from my lap and began to look over its pages again, clearly skeptical.

"I admit it looks like the real thing, Daddy, but I've seen people go to greater lengths than that for a laugh."

"A laugh?"

"Yes, Daddy, a laugh. For all we know, that book's just somebody's idea of a sick joke."

"But the handwriting—"

"Could be anyone's. I've never seen Wildman's handwriting. Have you?"

She'd done it again: asked another question we could only answer with silence.

Until, that is, Big Joe said, "No. But I know where we can find some people who have."

And he did, too.

Just northeast of the Capitol Building on Constitution Avenue, three Senate office buildings sit on opposite sides of First Street: the Russell, Dirksen, and Hart buildings. The Russell stands alone on the northwest corner; the Dirksen and Hart buildings are adjuncts of the same major complex on the northeast corner. It was in the Dirksen Building that we found the offices of Senator Graham Wildman.

I use the word "we" here only figuratively, because I was the only one who actually went in. Mo and Big Joe stayed in the truck outside. We'd all agreed the story we came up with would only fly with one person telling it, not three, so I was the one chosen to go in. My husband and daughter told me I had the best face for the job.

Fifty bucks a month on cosmetics, and apparently, all I have to show for it is the face of a liar.

"Can I help you?" Wildman's receptionist asked, finally managing to tear herself away from the phone. A pretty if somewhat cherubic redhead, she smiled, but only out of habit.

"Yes. I think I have something that belongs to Senator Wildman," I said, clutching my purse to my bosom like something that had fallen out of a Brink's truck.

"Something that belongs to the Senator? Like what?"

"Well, I'm not sure. But I think it's something he wrote."

"Something he wrote? I'm sorry, but I don't think I understand."

Her mouth was shrinking up in a pouty, cheerleader-like frown when the phone rang again. I used the interruption to look around a bit. Besides the one other person in the room—a middle-aged white man in a woeful powder-blue polyester suit, sitting in a chair behind me—there wasn't a whole lot to see. A few chairs, a wastebasket, and a watercooler; wall-mounted photographs of the Senator and, of course, the President of the United States. Between the two of them, Wildman took the better photograph; his hair was fuller and more naturally gray, and his smile seemed to promise more than a chicken in every pot. Behind that smile, however, if the allegations against him were true,

was a lech; a jerk who liked to fondle his way through the
female contingent of his staff the way mice like to nibble
their way through cheese.

"Now. You were saying this was something *written*?"
the receptionist asked, returning to our conversation.

"Yes." I nodded.

"May I see it?"

"Well . . ." I held my purse even closer to my chest. "It
looks kind of personal. I thought maybe—"

"You could give it to the Senator personally? I'm afraid
that wouldn't be possible. We're out of session at the moment, and the Senator's spending the break in his home
district in Delaware."

I used a prolonged silence to convey my disappointment.
She'd been skeptical from the first, and now she was
annoyed as well. I imagined that being a young woman on
Wildman's team had lately become stressful enough; she
didn't need strangers coming in off the street claiming to
have unnamed pieces of Wildman's personal effects, too.

"Look. I'm very sorry, but unless you're willing to leave
the item with me, there's really nothing else I can do. If it
looks like something that does indeed belong to the Senator, I promise you it will be returned to him. Unread." She
paused to put her smile back on. "Okay?"

I gave her a few minutes of my best *Black Woman Making Up Her Mind*, then opened up my purse and handed
her a single sheet of white paper.

It was a xeroxed copy of a page from the book we'd
found, just barely dark enough to be legible in most places.
It had been Joe's idea to make the copy of one of the book's
most innocuous pages, devoid of all proper names (other
than Wildman's) and sexual content. Joe said showing them
a "spicier" page in its entirety would be tipping our hand
unnecessarily. I had argued that they would need to see a

whole page of any kind to assess it properly, but Joe said no, a third of a page would be plenty.

He was right.

"Where did you get this?" Wildman's receptionist asked. She didn't sound particularly excited, but the photocopy definitely had her attention; the way she kept biting her lip as she read and reread it seemed to make that clear.

"I found it."

"You *found* it? Where?"

I told her I'd found it in one of the ladies' rooms at the F.B.I. Building, during a tour.

"The F.B.I. Building?"

"Yes. Does it look like something that might belong to the Senator?"

Instead of answering the question, she just stood up and said, "Wait right here a moment, will you please?"

She disappeared through a door behind her, taking the photocopied diary page along with her. Moving it up the ranks to the next level of command, no doubt. Someone in a blue (or brown?) suit with a small thicket of hair standing up at the front of his scalp, perhaps?

I held my breath and set my feet for a quick exit.

But the man the receptionist soon returned with was no one I knew. He had curly blond hair, and lots of it, and his style of dress was more college preppie than Wall Street: a crisp white dress shirt with the sleeves turned up, smart blue tie, and black trousers. The shirt wasn't soaked through with sweat, but I had the feeling it soon would be. He looked like a man who'd just found a live bomb under his bed.

"Hi. My name is Stuart Gross, Mrs. . . . ?" He held out his hand to shake and tried to smile, but he only looked more miserable.

"Washington," I said, accepting his hand. Not very

imaginative, I know, but when you're making things up as you go along . . .

"Mrs. Washington. I'm with Senator Wildman's staff. Gina here just showed me this document you say—" He suddenly noticed the man in the polyester suit sitting behind me and lowered his voice. "This document you say you found in the . . . F.B.I. Building, was it?"

"The F.B.I. Building, yes." I began whispering too. "In the ladies' room."

"Which one?"

"Which one?" I shrugged. Playing stupid. "I don't know which one. It was on the first floor, is all I know."

"I see. And this was all there was?" He waved the photocopy at me.

"Yes, sir. It was just that one page, sitting on the floor beneath the sink. I picked it up to throw it away and . . . well, I saw it had the Senator's name on it and thought it might be his. So I brought it here. I found out at the hotel where the Senator's office was, and came over to return it, just in case it's something important. Did I do the wrong thing?"

"Oh, no, no, no," Gross said, shaking his head to dismiss the idea. "In fact, you did the absolute right thing. You did splendidly."

"Then that *is* the Senator's?"

"Well . . ." He glanced briefly at Gina the receptionist, who was waiting as expectantly as I for his answer. "That's something only Senator Wildman himself can answer reliably, I'm afraid. But it looks like it could be, yes." He tried another smile, this one much better than the first. "So we'd like to hold on to this, if we could."

"Of course."

Steering me toward the door, suddenly in a hurry to get rid of me, Gross said, "As I said, it's probably nothing,

Mrs. Washington, but on the outside chance it isn't, is there somewhere the Senator can reach you later if he should decide to send you a little thank-you card, or something?''

Trying to avoid telling any more lies, I said, ''Oh, that's not necessary.''

''Please. The Senator would insist, I'm sure.''

What could I do? I told him my husband George and I were staying at the Four Seasons Hotel, room 104.

That's right. *George*.

''You get that, Gina?'' Gross asked, glancing back at the receptionist. ''Room one-oh-four at the Four Seasons.''

She nodded, scribbling on a notepad at her desk.

Opening the door for me, Gross all but pushed me out into the hall as he shook my hand again. ''Thank you again for coming, Mrs. Washington. It was really very thoughtful of you.''

''Oh, it was my pleasure. Tell—''

I stopped abruptly, catching sight of someone walking down the hallway to my left. Not more than three doors down, she had her arms full of fast-food bags and was headed my way, fast.

Stacy.

''Is something wrong, Mrs. Washington?'' Gross asked.

''Wrong? No, no. I was just going to say, please tell the Senator it was no problem at all. 'Bye!''

I turned right and started walking, as anxious to get out of that building as Gross was to see me do so. I never looked back to see if Stacy had noticed me. I never looked back to see if Gross had ever closed the door behind me. I never looked back at all.

And, praise God, nobody ever ordered me to stop and turn around.

''It's Wildman's diary all right,'' I said, joining my husband and daughter downstairs in the parking lot.

Big Joe said his requisite *"Jeez Looweez"*; then Mo said, "Mother, are you sure?"

"Little girl, if you'd seen the look on that man's face upstairs, you wouldn't ask me that. Seeing that page seemed to scare him half to death."

"Senator Wildman?"

"Of course not. Senator Wildman's in Delaware. I saw some youngster on his staff named Gross. Stuart Gross."

"And he said that was Wildman's handwriting?" Joe asked.

"No. Not exactly. He just said it could be."

"Then—"

"Joe, I just told you: It wasn't so much what he said, as what he *looked* like when he said it. That page really shook him up, believe me." I waited to make sure he needed no further convincing, then said, "And there's something else."

I told them about seeing Stacy in the hallway.

"Stacy? What was she doing there?" Mo asked.

"It looked like she was delivering somebody's lunch or something," I said.

"Did she see you?"

"No. At least, I don't think she did."

"Did you see where she was going?"

"No. I had to get out of there! Before she could see me and blow my cover."

"Your cover?"

I had hoped this subject wouldn't come up.

"Yes, Mo, my cover. What was I supposed to do, give Gross my real name?"

"I thought we agreed you weren't going to give them any name at all."

"I had no choice! The man asked me for my name, so I gave him one."

"And what name did you give him, Mother?" Mo asked me, already certain I'd said the wrong thing.

"Washington," I said, avoiding her gaze.

"Washington? *Martha* Washington?"

"No, of course not! Give me some credit for intelligence. All I gave him was a last name, Washington, and a phony hotel and room number." I started to chuckle. "Although I did tell him your father's name was George." I looked at Joe and completely broke up.

"You didn't," Mo said.

"Oh yes I did."

In less than five seconds, both she and I were bouncing around the truck's cab, hysterical. Big Joe watched us go at it for a minute, shaking his head, then fell in laughing right along with us.

When the three of us were finally able to regain our composure, Mo wiped her eyes and said, "Mother, I don't believe you."

"I know. I don't believe myself sometimes."

"Where were we, anyway?"

"Your crazy mother was telling us she didn't see where Stacy went," Joe said. "So we don't know if she was on her way to Wildman's office or not." He turned to me. "Isn't that right?"

I nodded. "Yes."

"But she was headed in that direction?"

"Yes. Definitely."

We all fell silent inside the truck, lost in our own thoughts. Eventually, Mo said, "I suppose her being in the building could just be a crazy coincidence. Don't you think?"

She looked at me first.

"Of course," I said.

We both turned to get Joe's vote, but all he did was shrug and say, "It could be."

Seeking a more definitive answer from him, Mo said, "But you don't think it was."

"I didn't say that. I just said it could be. Now, if she was there to see somebody in Wildman's office . . . that would be a different story. I'd say no way that was just a coincidence. But just being in the building?" He shook his head. "Who knows?"

Facing me again, Mo said, "I take it one person you didn't see up there was your friend in the blue suit. Otherwise, I expect you would have mentioned it by now."

"That's correct. I didn't see him."

"Of course, that doesn't prove anything. He could still be one of Wildman's people."

"He sure could," Joe said. "And now that we know what we've got is really a Wildman diary, I'd say that's exactly who he is. One of Wildman's people. A hired hand who's been looking to get the diary back for him."

"By any means necessary," I agreed.

"In other words, he's the one who murdered Emmitt," Mo said.

"That's what Vlade seemed to believe," Joe said.

"And now he knows we have the book," I said, the ugly thought only now occurring to me. "Or at least, he soon will, if he really is working for Wildman. Mr. Gross will see to that."

The three of us just sat there staring at each other, waiting for someone to convince us all that we hadn't just made a boneheaded mistake.

"Oops," Big Joe said.

We were driving back to the trailer park when a police

car pulled us over.

"What the hell is this?" Joe said when they put the lights on him.

"Joe, what did you do?"

"I didn't do anything! Something must be up."

"Oh Lord . . ."

An officer sidled up to Joe's side of the truck and asked to see his driver's license and registration. Joe asked him what the problem was, but to no avail; the cop just repeated his original request, leaving out the "please" this time. When Joe reluctantly complied, the lawman nodded thanks, then took the documents back to his car and immediately became embroiled in a long conversation with someone on the radio.

"I don't like the looks of this," Mo said.

"Neither do I," I agreed. Joe and I had been warned in no uncertain terms to keep our noses out of Eddie's case, and we'd just spent the last twenty-some hours totally ignoring that fact. If Detectives Dobbs and Early had made good on their promise to keep an eye on us . . .

"Look, what the hell's goin' on?" Joe barked. The cop who'd pulled us over had reappeared outside his window without my noticing.

"I'm afraid I'm going to have to ask you to follow me, Mr. Loudermilk. Unless you'd all prefer to ride in the car with me."

"Follow you? Follow you where?" Joe demanded.

"Not far. It'll be a five-minute ride, tops."

"That doesn't answer my question."

"No. It doesn't. But then, I didn't get any answers to my questions, either. I guess we'll both have to work in the dark on this one, sir."

"And if we refuse to go?" Joe asked, his voice rising.

"Then I'd be forced to formally arrest you and bring you along anyway," the cop said, for his own part maintaining some decorum. "My orders are to deliver you folks to a specified location, period. My preference is to do that peaceably, of course, but if you'd rather I did it the hard way . . ."

He put his right hand on the gun at his hip and stepped back, waiting.

He didn't have to wait long.

11

"Back here," Detective Bud Early said, waving us over.

He was standing at the end of a long, dark corridor in someone's bleak little Northeast D.C. apartment, away from the swarm of uniformed policemen and forensics officers that Joe, Mo, and I had suddenly found ourselves in the midst of upon passing through the front door. Early's partner, Dobbs, was right behind us, herding us forward toward the rear of the apartment like an angry sheepdog. She and a trio of poorly parked police cars had met us on the street outside, foreshadowing the grim scene to come, but she hadn't said two words since she'd thanked the cop who brought us here and sent him on his way. She just pointed in the direction she wanted us to go and told us to hold all our questions for later.

Early was standing in the open doorway of a tiny bedroom when the four of us reached him, dourly surveying the considerable wreckage within. That the room had recently hosted something akin to a war between two small countries was obvious; there wasn't an intact piece of furniture in sight. But that was only the second thing one noticed about the room. The first was the body sprawled out in the middle of it. A man, stretched out on the floor on his back, feet propped up on the bed, head turned up at an unnatural angle that allowed us a perfect view of the vacancy in his eyes.

Ahmed.

"Oh, my sweet Jesus," I said, stepping back out of the room.

"Yeah, I know. He's looked better, hasn't he?" Early said, striking a match to light a cigarette. He looked more like a man watching paint dry than a cop on the scene of a homicide.

"Who is it?" Mo asked, the only one among us who had never met the deceased.

Joe told her, in twenty words or less.

"Never mind who he is, sister," Early said, resenting the interruption. "Who the hell are *you*?"

"Their attorney," Dobbs said, having already had Mo introduced to her as such outside. "And their oldest daughter, too, if you can believe that. Name's Maureen Watts."

"You're pullin' my leg," Early said.

"Nope." Dobbs shook her head, then turned to Mo. "My partner, Bud Early."

"Pleased to meet you, counselor," Early said, though he clearly wasn't. He offered his hand to shake and Mo took it, hesitantly.

"Look, never mind the introductions," Big Joe said angrily. "You told us you were gonna hold that boy for questioning! What the hell was he doin' here?"

"He was here because this was home," Dobbs said.

"That's not what I'm askin', and you know it. I'm askin' what he was doin' out of jail."

"He made bail, Mr. Loudermilk. What do you think?"

"Bail? When?"

"Sometime just after noon today. Or don't you remember?"

Joe was almost too stunned to respond to that. "Excuse me?"

"Now wait just a minute," Mo said, leaping to her father's defense. "If you're suggesting my parents had anything to do with this—"

"That strikes you as farfetched, does it?" Early asked.

"It strikes me as impossible. They've both been with me all day today; neither one of them was ever anywhere near this place."

"I see." He flicked the ashes off the end of his cigarette onto the floor, watching them fall, then looked up at me. "Out seeing the sights, were you, Mrs. L.?"

"You don't have to answer that, Mother," Mo said.

"We were supposed to have an understanding," Dobbs said. "You and your husband were going to go back to your trailer park and stay there. Leave the police work to us professionals."

"That's not true. We never said we'd remain indoors," I said. "All we said was that we'd keep our noses out of your investigation."

"And you didn't think Ahmed Lee was part of our investigation. Is that it?"

"No! Joe—"

"All right, Detectives, show's over," Mo said. "You want to question my parents regarding this homicide, we'll be glad to meet you downtown, anytime you say. Otherwise . . ." She started to escort me back down the hall.

"Waitaminute, waitaminute," Joe said, staying where he

was. "We don't need to go downtown to talk! We can do all the talkin' we're gonna do to these two right here, right now!"

"Dad, *no*," Mo said firmly.

"Look. Why keep them in suspense? Let's just tell 'em everything we know about this thing, and get it over with."

Mo started to object again, but I shook my head to silence her, thinking I could see what Joe had in mind.

"You want to know what happened here, right?" my husband asked Dobbs. "Who killed Ahmed, and why."

"Yes."

"I don't have the slightest damn idea. You, Dottie?"

"I sure don't," I said earnestly. "You, Mo?"

I was afraid she was going to drop the ball, but she said, "Me? No, ma'am. Not me." She shook her head to prove it.

"You think this is funny?" Dobbs asked us, fuming. "Think again."

"You broke in here looking for that book you've been rambling about and Lee came in here and caught you," Early said. "Why don't you just admit it?"

"Because that's not what happened," I said.

"Bullshit."

"What?"

"I think you'd better watch your mouth, Detective," Big Joe said. His eyes looked like a pair of acetylene torches turned up full blast.

"Look. Nobody's saying you intended to kill him," Dobbs said to Joe, cutting in before her partner could push him any further. "In fact, we're both pretty sure you didn't. We think the two of you just got locked up, and you hit him a little harder than you meant to. That's all. A man your size against a man his size . . . It could happen very easily."

"Except that it didn't happen. Period," Mo said. "My parents weren't here. How many times do we have to say it?"

"You know we didn't do this," Joe said. "And you know who did. So why the hell are you hassling us instead of him?"

"Don't tell me. Let me guess," Early said. "You're talking about the Vlade man again, right?"

"Damn right I am."

"The man you claim was Lee's *friend* yesterday."

"Yes. But—"

"Lee threatened *you* with a gun, but it was his buddy Vlade that wiped him out, not you. Is that what you're saying?"

"He's saying we didn't have anything to do with this," I said firmly, tired of watching the cop bully my husband. "But if we had to guess who did, we'd say it was Vlade. It's a guess, that's all."

"And Vlade killed Lee over the book?" Dobbs asked.

"Yes. I mean, I guess so. I don't know."

"But I thought you said they thought *you* had the book."

"They did."

"Then why would Vlade kill Lee over the book if he thought you had it, and not him?"

It was a good question, and one I could only think to answer one way: "I don't know."

Dobbs and Early took turns eyeing us, as if trying to glare us into submission. "You beginning to understand our problem here, folks?" Early asked, looking about ready to explode. "Nothing you say makes sense. It can't be explained, and it can't be proven. Now, yesterday, that was a minor inconvenience, but today, it's a bona fide pain in the ass. Because today, we've got a dead man on our hands. Don't we?"

We didn't say anything.

Eventually, Mo said, "I'd like to speak to my parents in private for a moment. Would that be all right?"

Early turned away, disgusted, so Dobbs was left to answer for them both. "Go ahead. Just make sure not to touch anything."

At the other end of the hall, near the still-teeming living room, Mo, Big Joe, and I formed a tight huddle as Mo said, "I think maybe we should tell them about the book."

She looked at us expectantly, waiting for someone to agree with her, and was disappointed when no one did. "Look, if they find out about it later—"

"Let 'em," Joe said. "Later, the book might prove somethin'. Right now, it doesn't prove a thing."

"I agree," I said.

"Besides—we give it to 'em now, who knows what they'll do with it? Maybe they'd pursue it as a lead, and maybe they wouldn't. Long as we have it, we at least know somebody's putting it to good use."

"And what use is that, Dad?" Mo asked.

"I don't know, yet. But I'll think of something."

Mo shook her head, unconvinced. "I don't like it. Like the detective just pointed out in there, a man is dead. And counting Emmitt, that makes two. Whatever's going on here, somebody's playing for keeps, and the deeper we get involved in it, the better our chances of getting killed ourselves."

Uh-huh. Just as I thought. She was throwing the word "we" around like the three of us were attached at the hip. I'd told Joe this would happen, and now it had: The gate-crasher had become the master of ceremonies. There'd be no sending her home now, short of stuffing her into a box and shipping her FedEx.

"All the same, Mo, your father's right," I said, deciding

to scold her later. "We have no idea what those two in there would do with the book if we turned it over now. And if they decided to sit on it, or worse, pretend it never existed . . ."

"We'd be up the creek without a paddle. And so would your brother," Big Joe said.

"Yes, but—" Mo started to argue.

"But nothing," I said. "The bottom line is, I don't trust those two, and neither does your father. To get Eddie out of jail, somebody's going to have to connect that book we found today with Emmitt's murder, and I'd just as soon see us try to do it as them."

"Precisely," Joe agreed.

Mo fell silent, outnumbered and outvoted. "Okay. If that's what you want to do."

Joe and I both nodded at her, assuring her it was.

When we rejoined Dobbs and Early in the bedroom, the former said, "Well? Anybody have their memory refreshed?"

Mo shook her head. "I'm afraid there's nothing to remember. What we've told you from the start still stands, Detectives: None of us knows anything about this. End of story. You want to take us downtown to hear that officially, let's go."

She crossed her arms across her chest, just the way her father does, and Joe did the same, bursting with pride. Why we call the girl Mo instead of Little Joe, I'll never know; she's so much like her father, it's sickening.

"All right, counselor," Dobbs said bitterly. "You're free to go. For now. But what we told your parents yesterday goes double today: Go home, and stay home." She paused. "Please."

"And don't touch anything on your way out," Early said. He was not a happy camper.

We got out of there as fast as we could.

                           *   *   *

The first thing we did upon leaving Ahmed's apartment
was find a print shop. We weren't ready to turn Senator
Wildman's diary over to the police, but we weren't com-
fortable driving all over town with it under the driver's seat
of our truck, either, so we decided to duplicate a number
of its pages before hiding it in the safest place we could
think of: on board a Federal Express cargo plane. We
thought about mailing it to ourselves in D.C. in care of
General Delivery, but that was too obvious, so we sent it
same-day air to someone else instead, along with a letter
instructing the receiving party to do nothing with the plain-
wrapped parcel in the envelope but hold on to it for us for
a while.

To say that Mo didn't care for the person Joe and I decided to ship the book to would be a gross understatement.

"Dee? Mother, you can't be serious."

"Dee" is what we all call Delila, Mo's younger sister.

"Mo, this is nothing your sister can't handle," I said.

"Let me send it to someone in California. Please."

"We don't want it going to a stranger. It has to go to
someone we can trust."

"I'll send it to someone we can trust. I promise."

"I mean someone in the family, Mo. Someone we can
count on to do what we ask with the book, no matter
what."

"You mean, after reading it?"

"She's not going to read it."

"Hmph. That girl will be thirty pages into it before the
deliveryman's stepped off the porch."

There was some risk of that, it was true. Dee, who lives
in Colorado Springs, Colorado, is a reporter for the *Inside
Scooper*, the tabloid news magazine you see in all the su-
permarkets, and everything is a story waiting to happen as

far as she is concerned. The child has a curiosity factor of about 135 percent. Sending her a package essentially labeled ''Do Not Open Until Christmas'' could have been asking for trouble, and yet Joe and I were convinced no one would do a better job of guarding it with their life than she could.

Providing we promised her the full story later, of course.

''How did you know where to find me?'' Stacy asked.

We were sitting at a patio table in front of the Capitol Hill Deli, a sandwich shop and café on Constitution Avenue and Third Street Southeast, just outside the shadow of the Capitol Building itself. The lunch-hour rush had long since passed, and we'd found Stacy standing around inside, waiting for something to do.

''We called looking for you at Angus's and Eileen told us you were here,'' I said, after we'd introduced her to Mo.

''I see. So what's up?''

I wondered what, if anything, it meant that she didn't ask about Eddie.

''We saw you at the Dirksen Building today. Delivering sandwiches,'' I said.

''The Dirksen? Oh, yeah, sure. I was there earlier. So?''

''You were headed for Senator Wildman's office, it looked like.''

''Senator Wildman? Uh-uh.'' She shook her head. ''I didn't have anything for him today. I was on that floor making a delivery to Senator Beale, though.'' She frowned. ''Why?''

''Because we found the book we think got Emmitt killed,'' Big Joe said, no doubt to see what her reaction would be to the news.

''You did? Where?''

"In a bookstore called Get It in Writing," I said. "Ever hear of it?"

"I thought 'Get It in Writing' was the *title* of the book."

"Well, it turns out we were wrong about that. 'Get It in Writing' was just the name of the shop where Emmitt hid the book, disguised in a jacket from another book called *The Power of Modern Litigation.*"

Stacy thought about that a moment, then shrugged. "I don't get it," she said.

"That's because you haven't seen the book," Big Joe said.

"Or have you?" Mo asked.

"Look," Stacy said. "I don't know what you guys are talking about, but I am at work here. So if you don't mind getting to the point . . ."

"The point is, we have reason to believe the book we're talking about belongs to Senator Wildman," I told her. "And we think you might know how it eventually came into Emmitt's possession."

"Me? Why me?"

"Because you visit the Senator's office all the time. Don't you?"

"Do you mean, have I made deliveries there before? Of course. I've been to practically all the senators' offices, at one time or another. But if you think that grants me *access* to anything—"

"Let's just put it this way," Joe said. "Emmitt's buddy Vlade got his hands on the Senator's book somehow, and he doesn't have a job running sandwiches to every congressional office building in town. *You* do."

The young woman fell silent, her annoyance having turned to something infinitely darker. "Number one, delivering lunch to the members of a senator's staff generally gets me no farther than the receptionist's desk. I could no more get near one of the Senator's books than I could his favorite pair of pajamas. And number two, I don't know anybody named Vlade. I told you that two days ago."

"What about someone named Taz?" I asked. It was the first opportunity we'd had to ask the question since Ahmed had dropped the name.

"Taz?"

No matter what she said now, her eyes had already given us our answer: She knew the name.

"Yes. Taz," I said. "Do you know him?"

"What's he got to do with this?"

"The same thing Vlade does," Joe said. "Apparently, he and Taz are one and the same."

"You mean, Taz is Vlade?"

"You catch on fast," Mo said.

Just to make sure we were talking about the same person, I described the man we knew as Vlade for Stacy, before the look she turned on my daughter could turn into an argument.

"Yeah. That's him," she said.

"All right. So tell us about him," Mo said.

Stacy shrugged again. "There's really nothing to tell. He's some friend of Angus's who came by the house one day. I answered the door and told him Angus wasn't in. I haven't seen or heard of him since."

"He's a friend of Angus's?" I asked.

"That's what he said. And Angus acted like he knew who I was talking about when I told him about it later."

"How long ago was this?"

"I don't know. Two or three weeks ago, maybe. You think he's the one who killed Emmitt?"

"We aren't sure. But right now, that looks like a pretty safe bet."

"Where is Angus now?" Big Joe asked.

"Angus? He's on a run. But he should be back in a few minutes, it's almost quitting time."

"Quitting time?"

"Waitaminute, waitaminute," I said. "Are you saying Angus works here too?"

"Sure. He was here before I was. That's how I got the job. Angus recommended me."

"Then he makes all the same runs you do. To all the congressional buildings and such."

"Yes. But I already told you—"

"Yeah, we know," Joe said, cutting her off. "He could no more get his hands on one of the Senator's books than he could the Senator's favorite pair of pajamas."

"That's right. He couldn't." She paused a moment, then said, "By the way—you never said what kind of book of the Senator's you found."

"No. We didn't," Mo said.

Stacy just glared at her. For some reason, the brunette and my daughter were not exactly hitting it off.

"We don't mean to be secretive, Stacy," I said, "but the way things have been going lately, the less you know about the book, the better off you probably are. We may have told you more than it's safe for you to know as it is."

"More than it's *safe* for me to know? Come on."

"We kid you not," Joe said.

Stacy looked the three of us over, trying to decide whether or not it would be worth her while to push us on the subject, before finally realizing it wouldn't be. "So how's Eddie doing?" she asked instead.

Better late than never, I thought to myself.

"He's doing all right, considering," I said.

"I've been meaning to go see him. Maybe I'll go tomorrow."

"I'm sure he'd be glad to see you."

She nodded at me and grew quiet. We all did. We had come into this conversation expecting it to answer some of the more nagging questions regarding the Wildman diary, but here it had petered out to a decidedly anticlimactic end and what we had to show for it was next to nothing.

Time dragged on.

Finally, Stacy looked up and said, "Hey, here comes Angus now."

She was peering down the street to her left, but when the rest of us turned to follow her gaze, whatever had originally caught her attention was gone.

"That's funny," she said. "He turned off . . ." She was still looking off in the same direction, as if she couldn't quite believe what she'd just seen. Eventually, she turned to face us again and shrugged. "I thought he was coming in, but he kept going. Maybe he had another drop to make I didn't know about."

"Or maybe he saw us sitting here and decided not to stop," Mo said.

Stacy shrugged again, unable to deflect the suggestion any other way.

"Maybe he did," she said.

12

The first thing you see upon entering the Nation's Best trailer park in Arlington, Virginia, where we had Lucille hooked up, was the visitors' parking lot, adjacent to the manager's office. Since our arrival in D.C. five days ago, we had passed by the lot at least twice a day, never seeing anything in it worth mentioning. If you've seen one 1987 Pontiac Sunbird with Indiana plates, you've seen 'em all. But this time was different. This time we spotted an old friend there.

"Joe, look," I said as we cruised past the lot.

"I see it," he said.

A white Chrysler sedan, District of Columbia license plate GN5152.

"While the three bears are away, Goldilocks will play," Big Joe said. "Or so he thinks."

"What are you two talking about?" Mo asked, once more sitting between us in our truck's cab.

160

Joe pulled over to the side of the access road, where we were still far enough away that we could neither see our trailer nor be seen by anyone in its general vicinity, and we told her: The man Joe had chased halfway across the city of Alexandria yesterday was here, no doubt taking advantage of our absence to search Lucille for Wildman's diary.

"Okay. Time to call the cops," Mo said.

"Later," Joe said, opening his door to step out of the truck.

"What do you mean, *later*? Daddy, we have to call them now!" Mo cried as she and I rushed after him. He was headed straight for Lucille.

"We can take care of this ourselves," my husband said, turning on us. "Now, you and your mother go get back in that truck."

"No. If you go, we go."

"Mo, do what I say."

"No!"

It was always this way with these two. Joe snaps an order, Mo refuses to obey it; Joe reissues the order, Mo rejects it again. And then:

"Dottie, tell her to do what I say," Big Joe said.

Like that ever works.

"Joe, I think Mo is right," I said. "We don't know what that man might do, we go in there and surprise him."

"Yeah, well, he doesn't know what *I* might do either, he puts one scratch on my trailer. So it all balances out."

He started walking again.

From a distance, Lucille appeared perfectly normal, but when we closed upon her farther, we could see that her door was open a good three or four inches.

"No, I did not leave the door open again," I said to Joe, the instant he turned around to glare at me. I used to make that mistake all the time, but I don't anymore. Not since the time my doing so led Joe and me to find our son Bad Dog in our closet and a dead man on our toilet.

It's a long story.

"You two stay here," Joe said. "And this time, I don't want any arguments."

"Joe—"

I tried to catch his arm, but he was too fast. Mo and I could only watch as he slipped slowly up to Lucille's door, peered carefully inside, and then climbed into the trailer and out of sight.

"Mother, this is insane," Mo said, clearly distraught.

"Yes, it is," I admitted, in no better shape than she was.

Another long minute passed, marked by no sound or motion from Lucille.

"We have to go in there," Mo said.

"You're right. Let's go."

We eased our way over to Lucille's door, Mo leading and me following. We still hadn't heard a sound from within, or seen anything to indicate two men might be rolling about inside, locked in mortal combat. I didn't know if that was good or bad.

Mo reached the door first and peeked inside.

"I don't believe this," she muttered.

"What?"

She turned around to frown in my direction, then threw the door open and walked boldly inside.

Joe was sitting on the lounge with a tall, thin white man I'd never seen before, both of them chatting amiably. The stranger had a twenty-inch black skillet in his lap. At their feet, the government man Joe had meant to surprise lay stretched out on the floor, on his back, out cold. He'd gone back to his blue suit today.

The scene was completely surreal, and would have made

no sense to me whatsoever had I not caught the tail end of something the strange man with the skillet in his lap was saying to my husband as Mo and I came in. I hadn't caught much, but one word had stood out: "Limited."

It had taken him five days, but Big Joe had finally found himself another Airstream nut.

As I was to learn hours later, his name was Gerald Gibbons, of Tacoma, Washington, and he was the proud owner of a 1983 thirty-four-foot Airstream Limited. He had arrived at the trailer park only that morning, along with his wife, four children, and mother-in-law, and had spotted our Excella almost immediately upon pulling in. Naturally, he had made up his mind right then that he would come by and say hello just as soon as he got the chance, and when he finally did, he came upon our friend in the blue suit working on Lucille's door like a midnight man, trying to force his way inside. Gibbons backed off before being seen.

Now, most people at this point would have run to the nearest phone and called the police, but this was an *Airstream* crime Gibbons had just witnessed, you understand, and that of course made it an offense he was obligated to thwart *personally*. That's just the way Airstreamers are. If it's silver and has wheels, it's worth defending to the death, no matter whose name is on the registration slip.

And the folks at Mercedes-Benz think they know a thing or two about pride of ownership.

Anyway, Gibbons raced back to his trailer, retrieved his wife's largest skillet, and returned to defend Lucille's honor, just as our would-be vandal was getting her door open. The poor devil had only taken one step inside when Gibbons caught him from behind and coldcocked him, dropping him to the floor in a heap. Big Joe showed up immediately afterward, and yet another chapter in the history of the Loyal Order of Airstream Yahoos was born, God bless their little hearts.

Either Joe or Gibbons would have gotten around to checking our unwanted visitor for a pulse eventually, I'm sure, but Mo wasn't up to the wait, and neither was I. To us, the nasty bruise on the left side of his head had the look of something a fresh corpse might wear. Mo knelt down to put a tentative hand at his throat and let out a deep sigh.

"He's breathing," she said.

Gibbons was so relieved he almost blinked.

"See if you can find his wallet," I told Mo. "Quick, before he comes around."

Nodding, she peeled the man's coat back to get to his inside breast pocket . . . and exposed an automatic handgun of some kind, sitting snugly in a shoulder holster under his left arm. Not a good sign.

"Uh-oh," Mo said.

"I think you'd better hand me that," Joe said. Like he was talking about a thumbtack he was afraid we might step on.

Mo unsnapped the weapon from its holster and gently slid it free, treating it with the utmost revulsion. She laid it in her father's outstretched hand, then found the government man's wallet and flipped it open—to more bad news. A badge and a picture ID card, both belonging to one Harris Murphy of the United States Capitol Police. Not the District of Columbia Police Department—the United States Capitol Police.

"Well, I think I'll be off," Gibbons said, getting to his feet.

"Yeah. I think maybe you'd better be," Big Joe agreed, shaking his hand before walking him to the door.

"You won't mention that it was me who . . ." Gibbons

pantomimed the overhand frying pan swing he'd used on our unwanted guest.

"No, no, no. I'll take credit for that, don't worry."

"Joe, maybe you should have him call the police," I said, before Gibbons and his frying pan could get away completely.

"What for? The police are already here," Joe said.

"I know that, but—"

"I'd be happy to make the call if you want," Gibbons said.

"Not just yet, Mr. Gibbons," Mo broke in, "but thanks."

I turned to glower at her as Gibbons made good his escape. "Mo!"

"Mom, everything's under control. The man's unarmed, and if he gives us any trouble—"

"Daddy'll take care of it. Tell her, Turtle," Joe said. He was grinning like a kid.

I showed him a brief frown before turning a bigger one on Mo. "You've got an awful short memory, little girl. Just two minutes ago, you were all for calling the police. Now you change your tune. If it were just your father and me here, you know what you'd be saying. 'Oh, Mother, you've got to call the police! That's a *policeman* you and Daddy are fooling with! Do you want to get yourselves *killed*?' "

Mo started laughing.

"But because *you're* here to protect us, it's suddenly okay to take chances. To throw caution to the wind."

"Mother—"

"You're a hypocrite, Maureen Loudermilk. You want people to do as you say, not as you do."

She punched me playfully on the arm. "I am not a hypocrite! And he's waking up.'' She pointed at the man on the floor. ''Daddy . . .''

''I see him,'' Joe said, moving over to put himself between us and the plainclothes police officer beginning to stir at our feet.

Rubbing the back of his head with his right hand, Harris Murphy rolled up to a sitting position on the floor and tried to focus his eyes on the three of us, blinking and squinting. Struck by a sudden thought, he reached inside his coat for his gun . . . and realized it wasn't there. Finding it in Joe's hand, pointed down at the floor, seemed to help him clear the cobwebs almost instantly.

''Who hit me?'' he asked, of no one in particular.

Big Joe told him he had done it, just as he'd promised Gibbons he would.

''With what? A Toyota?'' Murphy was still rubbing his head and grimacing.

''A frying pan,'' Joe said.

''A frying pan?''

''Yeah. You want to tell us what you were doing in our trailer, Officer''—Joe consulted Murphy's wallet again—''Murphy?''

Murphy started to reach inside his coat again, then caught himself; the wallet he'd just been reminded of was in Joe's hand. ''Then you know I'm with the Capitol Police,'' he said.

''I know that's what it says here. But that doesn't answer my question.''

''Look. Tell you what. You give me my gun and wallet back now, and I'll forget all about charging you with assault against a police officer. Okay?'' He started to get up.

''Mo, go call the police,'' Joe said.

As Mo started for the door, Murphy waved her off and

said, "Whoa, whoa, whoa! I don't think you understand. I *am* the police."

"Great. Then you won't mind us calling a few of your buddies down here to help you haul us in, will you?" He turned and said, "Go on, Mo."

Again our daughter started to do as she was told, and again Murphy threw his hands up to stop her. "Okay, okay! You've made your point. You don't want any cops down here, and neither do I."

"I didn't think you would," Joe said.

Murphy went back to rubbing his head. "Do you have the book?" he asked, without bothering with any preamble.

It took Joe a moment to decide how to answer that. "What book is that?"

"Come on, Mr. Loudermilk. Emmitt Bell's book. What else?"

"Be more specific," I said.

"I wish I could be, Mrs. Loudermilk, believe me. But I can't. All I know about the book is that Bell intended to use it to blackmail a member of the U.S. Senate."

"And who would that be?" Mo asked him.

"I'm afraid I'm not at liberty to say," Murphy said.

"In that case, we don't know what book you're talking about," Big Joe said.

"Now, wait a minute—"

"Face it, Officer Murphy. You want answers, and so do we. You've been following us around for four days now, so I suspect we don't have to tell you what our interest in all this is. We want our son out of jail, and out from under the murder charge he's facing. We don't give a damn about the rest. That means if you can help us, we'll be more than happy to help you. Otherwise . . ." Joe shrugged. "You can get the hell out of my house right now."

Murphy studied my husband's face for a long minute,

considering his options. When it finally occurred to him he didn't really have any, he said, "Bell was trying to blackmail Dick Meany."

I thought my jaw was going to hit the floor. It was Meany's so-called antidisclosure bill that Eddie and his friends had come to Washington to fight.

"Dick Meany?" Joe said, no less surprised than I was.

"That's right," Murphy said, his curiosity piqued by our reaction to the name. "You were expecting someone else?"

We had been, of course, and there wasn't much point in denying it.

"Frankly, yes," Joe said.

"Who?"

Joe glanced in my direction, looking for help, then said, "Graham Wildman."

"Graham Wildman?" Murphy seemed as surprised to hear that name as we'd been to hear Meany's. "What's he got to do with this?"

"We don't know. Maybe nothing. But it's his book you say Emmitt intended to blackmail Senator Meany with."

"Wildman's book?"

"Yes. At least, it appears to be his."

"It appears to be? Then you *do* have it?"

"Not here," Joe said, without elaborating.

"What kind of book is it?" Murphy asked.

"We'll tell you that when you've told us what you're doing here," I said, determined to keep this trade-off of information in balance.

"What I'm doing here? I was looking for the book, of course."

"That's not what I mean. What I mean is, what's *your* interest in all this? Who are you working for?"

"Look at the ID again, Mrs. Loudermilk. I'm with the U.S. Capitol Police. We're the police force on Capitol Hill.

We handle all matters of congressional security.''

"Such as blackmail threats against U.S. senators," Mo said.

"Among other things, yes."

"Then you're working for Senator Meany," Joe said.

Murphy nodded. "That's right. Early last week, his office got a call from someone saying they had a book of some kind that could end his political career, and the Senator came to me to get to the bottom of it. Last Monday, he received a second call instructing him to meet with the blackmailer at a neutral site, where the blackmailer would supposedly describe the nature of the book in question—only I went in the Senator's place."

"And found out Emmitt was your blackmailer."

"Yes."

"This meeting you're talking about—it wouldn't have been at the Zoo Room, would it?"

"That's right. What a dump."

"Then you were there the night Emmitt died too," I said.

"I was there, yes. But I didn't kill him, if that's what you think."

"But you know who did."

"No. I'm afraid I don't. I'd like to get your son off the hook, Mrs. Loudermilk, really. But I can't. I spent most of the evening watching Bell, all right, but I didn't witness his murder. I'm sorry."

"How did you manage to miss that?" Mo asked suspiciously.

Showing some embarrassment, the policeman said, "I got distracted. Some idiot who'd had too much to drink started shoving his girlfriend around, and dropped her right on top of my table. Next thing I know, I'm in the middle of a six-minute brawl. By the time I got out from under, Bell was gone. Dead in the back alley."

"You were the one who found him?" Joe asked.

"Not officially. But I was the first one there after the fact, yeah."

"Then it was you who lifted his wallet."

"I didn't have much choice. The book wasn't on him, and that meant I'd have to go looking for it. So . . ." He shrugged.

"You started breaking into his various residences."

"And following us around," I added.

"Yes, ma'am," Murphy said. "You seemed to be following a hotter trail than I was, so after a while, I thought it might be wise to hitch my horse to your wagon. And it looks like I was right. You found the book before I did, didn't you?"

If he expected an answer to that, he didn't get one.

"Come on now, people," he said. "I leveled with you, now it's your turn to level with me. We're trying to help each other out here, remember?"

Joe and I both looked to Mo to make the call. She seemed about to protest, then thought better of it and merely nodded her head, giving us the go-ahead.

We told Murphy everything we knew. It was a risky thing to do, but we did it.

When we were done, Murphy asked us how much of the Wildman diary we had read.

"Not a whole lot," Joe told him. "Mostly, we just skimmed through it."

"Anybody see any mention of Senator Meany?"

We all looked at each other. No one had.

"Are you sure?"

"No. We're not sure. Are you sure you don't know anything about Ahmed's murder?"

It was a question that had to be asked; *somebody* had killed Ahmed, and we couldn't think of any reason for

Vlade—or Taz, as we were now calling him, since Stacy had told us that was really his name—to have done it.

"Ahmed. He was the guy you said was with this Taz character at the crack house?"

"That's right."

Murphy shook his head. "Don't know the man. And apparently, I never will, huh?"

If he was lying, he was doing a masterful job of it.

"So when can I see it?" he asked.

"The diary?"

"If that's what it is. Yes. The diary."

We hadn't told him exactly where it was, just that we'd stashed it in a safe place and it would take some time to retrieve it.

"You can see the book itself tomorrow," Joe said. "But if you want, you can see some copies we made of a few pages right now."

"You made a copy?"

"Not of the whole book. Just of ten or so pages." He turned to our daughter. "Go get them, Mo."

Mo went out to the truck.

When she returned, Murphy looked the pages over in silence, pausing only to scratch at the top of his forehead and the wayward clump of hair that resided there.

"When can I see the rest?" he asked, finally.

"I told you," Joe said. "Tomorrow."

"Tomorrow? What time tomorrow?"

"That depends. And please, don't ask what on." My husband didn't want to have to explain how much trouble we might have trying to get Dee to send the book back without allowing her to photocopy every page first.

"Well? Is it a Wildman diary or not?" Mo asked Murphy.

"It's hard to say. Definitely looks and reads like one, though."

"But?"

"But if it is, I'd sure as hell like to know how our Mr. Taz got hold of it."

"You don't think there's any chance Wildman himself gave it to him?" Big Joe asked.

"Wildman? For what? So he could use it to blackmail Meany?" Murphy shook his head again. "Not a chance. The senators aren't friends, exactly, but they aren't archrivals, either. They're both conservative Republicans who vote along much the same lines. People on the Hill reserve blackmail for members of the other camp, Mr. Loudermilk, not casual acquaintances in their own. Besides—if just half of what they say is supposed to be in 'em is true—a Wildman diary could put a hurt on a lot more careers in this town than Senator Meany's. A lot more. Putting one in the hands of a blackmailer just to destroy one man would be like using a stick of dynamite to get rid of a loose tooth."

"But if Wildman didn't give it to him, who did?" I asked.

"I don't know. Other than Wildman himself, there couldn't have been that many people with access."

"What about Angus? He might have had access."

"Angus Berry? What, because he delivered sandwiches to Wildman's office every now and then? Not likely, Mrs. Loudermilk."

"But—"

"I'm not saying it couldn't happen. I'm just saying I doubt it very seriously."

"Why don't we go talk to him?" Joe asked. "Just to be sure?"

"We? We who?"

"We four. The three of us, and you."

Murphy shook his head emphatically. "That's out of the question, Mr. Loudermilk. If I decide to talk to Angus Berry, I'll do it alone."

"Oh, please. Not again," I said.

"Not again, what?"

"Not another 'Keep your noses out of police business or we'll run you in' speech. That's what."

"Mrs. Loudermilk—"

"Look. We're in this for the duration, do you understand? We have a job to do—to clear our son of Emmitt Bell's murder—and we're not going to get out of *anybody's* way until we do it. Not yours, not the M.P.D.'s, not anybody's. You want to keep this business about the diary quiet? Help us get our son out of jail. Otherwise, lock us up and throw away the key. Right now. And keep an eye out for us on *Inside Edition*. And *Sixty Minutes*. And *Twenty/Twenty*. And—"

"Okay, okay. I get the point."

He was mad, but I could tell it wouldn't last. He took a few seconds to calm himself, then looked at Joe and said, "How long have you two been married?"

"Thirty-four years," Joe said. "And yes, she's always been like this."

"Wow," Murphy said.

And we women think men have no sense of humor.

"Mom, I don't understand."

"Dee, I don't have time to explain it right now. Just do as I say and send the package back as soon as you receive it. *Without opening it.*"

"You sent me a package Federal Express, but you don't want me to open it."

"That's right."

"Why? What's going on?"

"I'll tell you all about it later, Dee."

"This has something to do with Bad Dog, doesn't it?"

"No. You leave your poor brother out of this. I have to get off the phone now. Did you write down the name and address I gave you?"

"Mom, don't do this to me. Please."

"Dee, did you get the address?"

"Yes, I got it." She repeated the address of the Nation's

Best trailer park and the name of its manager exactly as I had given them to her. "Mom—"

"I have to go now, Dee. I'm sorry. Your father and I both know you won't let us down."

"But—"

"Love you, baby. 'Bye!"

I hung up the phone.

"I told you not to send it to that girl," Mo said, shaking her head. She was standing at the pay phone right beside me, where she'd easily eavesdropped on the whole conversation. Big Joe and Harris Murphy were waiting a few yards away in our truck and Murphy's car, respectively.

"Stop it, Mo. She's going to do fine," I said.

But I couldn't even look her in the eye when I said it.

Angus took the Fifth.

Or at least, he thought about it, before the cop we'd brought along started scaring the living hell out of him.

He hadn't come home until well after ten o'clock, but we were there waiting for him when he walked in. At Mo's suggestion, we'd parked our truck around the block and out of sight, so as not to tip him off we were there. Maybe he would have come in anyway, but we doubted it.

Eileen and Stacy left us alone in the living room to talk to him. We did most of the talking to start; then it was his turn. Though, like I said, Murphy had to lean on him a little to get him going.

"I think I'd better call my lawyer," Angus said at one point.

"Sure," Murphy said. "If that's what you want to do. But I think it's only fair to warn you, that's going to change things a little."

Angus had to think about that for a minute. "What do you mean?"

"I mean that right now, I don't have any reason to go hard on you. You haven't pissed me off yet. But you go running to your lawyer, and I find out later you're even the least bit dirty, sonny boy, I'm going to jump on your chest with both feet. Me, and all my friends on the Hill."

He didn't embellish the threat with a smile. He just sat there and waited for Angus to decide what to do about it, as did Mo, Big Joe, and I.

"Okay," Angus said, almost mouthing the word more than speaking it.

"Tell us about your friend Taz," Murphy said.

"Taz is not *my* friend. He was a friend of Emmitt's. I'd like to get that straight right now."

"Emmitt?"

"That's right. I hardly even know the guy."

"Why do you know him at all?"

Angus sighed deeply and said, "He and Emmitt shared a jail cell together once. Emmitt called me to come bail him out, and I did. It just happened Taz was getting sprung around the same time. I met him then. Emmitt introduced me to him at the station."

"So what's his full name?"

"I have no idea. Emmitt just called him Taz. I figured that was short for 'Tasmanian,' because he kind of looks like the Tasmanian Devil. You know—the cartoon character."

That sounded logical to me; there was indeed a resemblance between the two.

"If Taz was Emmitt's friend, why did he come here looking for you?" Murphy asked.

"What?"

"You heard me. He came here a few weeks ago looking for you. You don't remember?"

"No. I mean—"

"Come on, son. Do you, or don't you?"

"Yes. I do. It's just that . . . I never found out what he wanted with me. He never came back to say."

"Excuse me?"

"It's the truth. He only came looking for me that one time."

"So why didn't you just call him back?" Murphy asked.

"Call him back? You mean on the phone?"

"No, on a ham radio. Of course I mean the phone."

"I didn't have his number. I told you, I don't know the guy."

"He didn't leave his number when he came by?"

"No."

"And you didn't ask Emmitt for it?"

"No. I keep telling you, I didn't know the man, and I didn't want to. Whatever he wanted with me, I knew it was trouble, so I just ignored his visit and hoped he wouldn't come back. And he never did, like I said."

Murphy took a while to ask his next question, presumably to further play on Angus's nerves. "You have any idea how he might have gotten hold of something belonging to Graham Wildman?"

"Graham Wildman? The senator?"

"Senator Graham Wildman, yes," Murphy said, holding fast to his withering patience.

"Something like a book, you mean?"

"How did you know I was talking about a book?"

"I didn't. But Mr. and Mrs. Loudermilk here have been looking for a book for days now. I just thought—"

"We're digressing, Mr. Berry. My question was, how could Mr. Taz have gotten hold of something belonging to Senator Wildman? Can you tell us that?"

Angus made a show of thinking about it. "I don't know," he said. "Why ask me?"

Murphy let a long silence convey how little he cared for that response. "Should I ask the question again?"

Angus wasn't looking so good. Murphy had him sweating bullets.

"He may have gotten it from Carol Dunne," Angus eventually said.

"Carol Dunne?"

The name meant nothing to me, but it obviously meant something to Murphy. Before I could ask him about it, however, Mo did it for me.

"Who is Carol Dunne?" she asked.

We'd been told to let the lawman do all the talking here, and up to now we'd done just that, but Murphy gave Mo a dirty look just the same, as if this were the seventeenth interruption he'd had to endure and not the first.

"Carol Dunne is Wildman's chief press-relations officer," he said.

Right on cue, Big Joe mumbled a barely audible "Jeez Looweez."

Murphy turned his attention back to Angus. "What makes you think he got it from Carol Dunne?"

Angus shrugged, being forced to talk about something he was clearly reluctant to discuss. "I saw them together once."

"Where?"

"In the Dirksen Building. Coming out of Senator Wildman's office."

"When was this?"

"About a month ago. Maybe more, I'm not sure."

"Before Taz came here to see you?"

"Yes. Before that."

"It was just the two of them?"

"Yes."

"And you're sure they were together? They couldn't

have just been leaving the office at the same time?"

"No. They were together. She was talking to him as they went down the hall."

"What were they talking about?"

Angus shook his head. "I don't know what they were talking about. I couldn't really hear them. I was at the other end of the hall."

"Then how—"

"She was looking right at him and doing a lot of gesturing. That's how. You were going to ask me how I knew she was talking to him, right?"

Murphy just looked at him. I had the feeling he was trying to decide whether Angus's last reply was flippant enough to warrant a backhand or two. Eventually, all the cop did was ask another question.

"Did Emmitt know about this?"

That stopped Angus cold for a moment. "About Taz being with Carol Dunne?" he asked, like there was one chance in a million Murphy could have been talking about something else.

"Yes. Did you tell him you'd seen them together?"

After a long pause: "No."

"No?"

"I mean, I might have mentioned it, I guess."

"You guess."

"Okay, I told him. Why not? I thought it was weird, those two being together, so I told him about it. I thought maybe he'd know what was up between them, but he didn't. He seemed just as surprised to hear about it as I was."

"And then?"

"And then, what? That's all I know."

"Emmitt didn't look Taz up later to ask him about his meeting with Dunne?"

"If he did, I never heard about it. Emmitt didn't tell me, and I didn't ask. I wanted no part of that guy—how many times do I have to tell you that?"

I thought Angus had finally earned his backhand, but Murphy didn't move. He simply turned to Mo, Big Joe, and me and asked, "You folks have any questions you'd like to ask Mr. Berry?"

"I do," I said, leaping into the breach. To Angus, I said, "Why didn't you tell the police all this?"

"I thought I just did," Angus said.

"I'm not talking about Officer Murphy here, and you know it. I'm talking about the detectives who've been investigating Emmitt's murder."

"If they had asked any of these questions, Mrs. Loudermilk, I would have answered them. But they didn't. It's as simple as that."

"You didn't think the information was worth volunteering?"

"No. It wasn't relevant to anything. Why would I volunteer it?"

"What do you mean, it wasn't relevant to anything? Taz—"

"Taz was a *friend* of Emmitt's, Mrs. Loudermilk. Not an enemy. He's bad news, yeah, but he's not the one who was threatening to kill Emmitt Monday night. Is he?"

He could have slapped me in the face and affected me less. Of all Eddie's friends, he had shown the least faith in our son's innocence, and yet, until this moment, I hadn't realized how thoroughly convinced of Eddie's guilt he was. He was Eddie's friend, not mine, and yet Eddie himself could not have possibly felt more disappointed and betrayed.

"You're wrong about Eddie, Angus," I said. "You wait

and see." It was all I could say without completely losing my cool.

"I hope you're right, Mrs. Loudermilk. But I doubt it."

He didn't even walk us to the door.

"Sorry to change the deal on you, folks, but you're gonna have to let me take it from here. Alone," Murphy said.

The four of us were sipping coffee in a crowded downtown McDonald's, having met there at Murphy's suggestion. He'd said of all the restaurants in Washington, D.C., this was the last one likely to be serving someone he didn't want to see at this late hour.

"Not so fast," Mo said.

"Look, this is not negotiable. You want me to help you, you're gonna have to trust me on this and back off."

"Why? Why should we back off?" I asked.

"Because if what Berry just told us is true, the game just changed. Carol Dunne is the big leagues, Mrs. Loudermilk. If she's really involved in this thing, you people are in way over your head. And for that matter, so am I."

"Then we're all in the same boat together."

"No, ma'am. We're not. You people are outsiders here. I'm not. I can see things coming you never would. And I have resources to call upon that you don't. If you take a seat and let me do my job, I'll get to the bottom of this thing. I promise you."

"Getting to the bottom of this thing is not necessarily our concern," Big Joe said. "Clearing our son of the charges against him is."

"I understand that," Murphy said.

"Do you? I wonder."

Joe gave him a hard look, using his eyes to deliver the

message that we needed some convincing if he wanted us to trust him with Eddie's life.

"I'll find out who killed Emmitt Bell. You have my word on it," Murphy said. He held out his hand for Joe to shake.

Joe looked at me before taking it, asking for my blessings.

"You have to keep us informed," I told Murphy. "Every step of the way."

"I'll do the best I can," Murphy said, trying to be non-committal. "And you three have to go underground. I'm talking about the lowest possible profile. I don't want any of you talking to *anyone* about this."

"Including the police?" I asked.

"I said anyone, Mrs. Loudermilk. That includes the M.P.D., yes."

"But—"

"Look, don't worry. I've got you covered. Just do as I say, and everything will be fine."

Just as Joe had looked to me for advice, I now looked at Mo.

She shrugged and said, "It sounds kind of fishy to me, but if he says he'll back us up . . ." She shrugged again.

Our daughter, the legal expert.

"Okay," Joe said, finally taking the cop's hand.

"But you've only got until Tuesday morning," I said.

"Tuesday morning? Now, waitaminute," Murphy said, shaking his head. "I didn't say anything about working under a deadline."

"No deadline, no deal," Mo said. This time she'd spoken like a lawyer, not a daughter, and Murphy couldn't help but notice the difference.

"Hell. Whatever you say," he said after a brief moment of indecision. "Three days with you all out of my hair should be plenty."

Out of his hair? Out of what *hair?* I thought to myself. But I didn't say it.

I didn't have the nerve.

"I hope we're doing the right thing," Mo said.

We were pulling into the trailer park again, only this time it was as dark and quiet as a cemetery. Ahead, yellow lights shone in but a handful of trailer windows, flickering like lonely candles against the stiff wind of night. The clock on our dash told us it was just a few minutes past one a.m.

"You heard the man. The game's changed," Joe said as he parked the truck. "It was dangerous before; now it's potentially fatal. Whatever chance we had of doing Eddie any good by ourselves is gone. We need help, and we might as well get it from the one person who's offering it: Murphy."

"If he's offering it for the right reasons, you mean."

Joe didn't ask her to explain that; he didn't have to. He knew as well as I did what she meant. The second Murphy told us who Carol Dunne was, we'd all understood that we no longer had a prayer of getting Eddie out of jail on our own; the forces we were up against had become too great. It was one thing to remain in the hunt while Graham Wildman's involvement in Emmitt's murder was little more than a distant possibility, and quite another now that it seemed all but a certainty. We'd done all we could by ourselves; the time had come to throw in with a cop.

So we had.

The question now was, had we thrown in with the right one?

It was something to think about as we approached Lucille's door. Murphy had fixed it so it would no longer lock, but Joe had managed to rig it so it would at least latch closed. And that's the way we had left it when we'd been here last, pulled tight and appearing secure. Imagine our surprise to find it no longer thus.

"Oh, no. Not again," Joe said wearily.

The door was standing open by two or three inches, just as it had been earlier in the day. The interior of the trailer beyond was pitch-black and silent.

"Don't go in there, Daddy," Mo said sternly.

"She's right, Joe," I said. "Let's just turn around and get out of here."

But my husband had already heeded the call of retreat once today, and like most men, that was his limit. He pushed open the door and went inside.

"Joe!"

He found the lights and turned them on. Detectives Dobbs and Early were standing inside, scowling as if we were the trespassers and they were the trespassed-upon. Mo seemed surprised, but Joe and I were just relieved; we'd been expecting Taz.

Our relief didn't last long, though. Just long enough for one of the two cops to speak.

"Where's Eddie?" Dobbs asked.

Proving that a long day had only been the prelude to an even longer night.

──── 14 ──

They told us Eddie had escaped from jail.

Details were still sketchy, but from what they'd been able to ascertain so far, he'd gotten out in a hospital laundry truck early Friday afternoon, hidden inside one of the bags. The guard who was supposed to have searched the truck and an inmate hospital orderly were being held as his accomplices. Dobbs said Eddie had been preaching his special brand of political dissent to every guard and inmate who would listen since his first five minutes at the prison, winning more converts in four days than Gandhi won in a lifetime, and the young men who had assisted him were among the most zealous—and gullible—of his followers. To hear them tell it, Dobbs said, they hadn't broken a suspected murderer out of jail—they'd freed a political prisoner. Yet another proud young black man done wrong by the racist American legal system. Falsely accused, arrested without cause, and unjustly incarcerated.

Oh, brother.

Of course, my initial reaction to all of this was one of total disbelief. Why would Eddie escape? Dobbs and Early were convinced he had done it because he was guilty as hell, as they'd both thought all along, and was looking to avoid an almost certain lifetime of imprisonment. I knew better. I knew Eddie was innocent. But I also knew he had a martyr complex, and a lawyer he had shown little faith in, and two parents and a sister who were worrying him to death with their amateurish attempts to help him, and . . .

On second thought, maybe I could see why he would try to escape after all.

Anyway, Dobbs and Early had gotten word of Eddie's daring breakout late, but when it came they'd had no problem deciding where to start looking for him first. At Mom and Dad Loudermilk's, of course.

I'd say the interrogation they put us through that night was for us akin to talking to a wall, except that a wall doesn't ask you to repeat yourself every time you say something. The expression "a broken record" doesn't mean anything anymore, what with the advent of compact discs, but that's what this conversation sounded like all the same: a phonograph needle skipping back on itself, playing the same musical track over and over again.

First Dobbs: *Do you know where Eddie is?*
No.
Have you seen him today?
No.
Do you know where he might be hiding?
No.
Then Early: *Do you know where Eddie is?*
No.
Have you seen him today?
No.

Do you . . .

And so on, and so forth. First at the trailer park inside Lucille, then downtown inside the same stale interrogation room we'd occupied before. They brought us in one at a time, they brought us in all together. The questions never changed, save for a synonym here and there. When they'd ask us individually how we'd spent our day, we couldn't help but contradict ourselves some; we'd had no opportunity to discuss how we would all respond to such questions. But we Loudermilks aren't stupid; we all just decided to stick as close to the truth as possible without mentioning the Wildman diary, or anything pertaining to it. In other words, we told them where we'd been, but not what happened when we got there.

We didn't fool them for a minute, but we didn't hang ourselves either.

In the end, they gathered us together one last time, to say their good-byes and issue a final word of caution.

"Playtime's over, people. This isn't funny anymore," Early said.

"You're hiding something, and we all know it," Dobbs said. "And frankly, I think it's Eddie."

"You think you're doin' him a favor, but you're not. And you're screwin' yourselves out of the rest of your lives."

"What my partner's telling you is, we find out you knew where Eddie was all along, we're gonna see you do more time than he does."

"Exactly," Early said. "Hell, I'll even show you to your cells myself."

A resounding silence fell over the room as they waited for somebody, *anybody*, to break down and tell them what they wanted to hear.

"Well?" Early demanded. "Doesn't anybody have anything to say?"

"I have something to say," Big Joe said. Mo and I turned, surprised. "Whatever happened to good cop, bad cop?"

Dobbs and Early were struck mute by the question.

"One of you guys is supposed to be nice to us. Who do I see to complain about you both being jerks at the same time?"

I thought the top of Early's head was going to come off and Dobbs might grind her front teeth into powder. The former's face looked like a coal in a barbecue pit, and you could see every muscle in the latter's jaw.

"Don't push it, Mr. Loudermilk," Early said when he'd finally found his voice again.

Which is generally what you say when you want my hardheaded husband to come at you with both guns blazing.

This time, however, Joe changed the script. He actually stopped pushing.

You could hear Mo's and my common sigh of relief in the next county.

I didn't sleep a wink.

But it was some consolation that no one else did either. Big Joe might have dozed off for an hour or so, Mo for half of that. Three people, two separate beds, same basic result: insomnia. Because whatever the truth was behind Eddie's escape, he was still out on the street, by now the subject of a considerable manhunt. What would he do if they found him? Run? Fight? Or surrender peacefully?

We didn't know.

So we spent the night talking, worrying, and praying. Trying to somehow reach across the void between us to deliver a message we needed him to hear: *Be smart*; *be careful*; *be safe*.

Morning came to bring more of the same. We showered, we dressed, and we worried. There was nothing else we could do. We'd made a deal with Murphy to let him do the detecting for a while, and we had to abide by it. It had been the right thing to do then, and it was the right thing to do now, Eddie's escape notwithstanding. Still, the temptation to go looking for Eddie was strong. Not that we knew of more than one place to look.

"If you've called to ask if we've seen Eddie, Mrs. Loudermilk, the answer is no," Eileen said. I'd called Angus's home immediately after breakfast, and she'd answered the phone.

"You sound as if you've been asked that question before," I said.

"As a matter of fact, I have. We've been talking to the police all morning."

"Detectives Dobbs and Early?"

"The same ones who were here before, yes, ma'am."

"And none of you have seen or heard from Eddie?"

"No. We haven't. I believe I just told you that."

"I know what you told me, young lady, but—"

"Look, Mrs. Loudermilk, we don't want to see Eddie get hurt any more than you do. If we'd seen or heard from him, we would've told him to turn himself in."

"And if he refused to do that? What would you do then? Turn him in yourself, right?"

She didn't have a ready answer for that.

"Eileen, listen to me. The boy's your friend, but he's our son. We don't want to lose him. All I ask is that you call us first if you hear from him. Can you promise me you'll do that? Please?"

I didn't think I was asking that much, but the time it

took Eileen to answer suggested she disagreed with me.
"Yes, Mrs. Loudermilk. I promise."

It wasn't the kind of promise you take to the bank, but
it was obviously all she was up to offering. So I took it,
thankful for small favors.

Kozy dropped in on us just before noon. He'd left half
a dozen messages for us with the trailer park manager the
day before, but we'd never gotten around to calling him.
We figured we could guess what it was he wanted to talk
about, so why bother?

The walking smile was openly relieved to discover we'd
already heard the bad news. Delivering it himself would
have required him to stop grinning for a moment, and the
thought of that must have disturbed him deeply. Maybe his
heart would survive the shock, and maybe it wouldn't.

"What made him do it, Kozy?" Big Joe asked him.

"I wish I could answer that, Mr. Loudermilk, but I can't.
I don't know why he did it."

"Did something happen to him in there? Did he get into
a fight, did someone threaten his life, anything like that?"

"Not that I'm aware of. No, sir."

"You didn't tell him about what happened to us at the
crack house by any chance, did you?" I asked, the thought
having just occurred to me.

"Well . . ." His smile didn't go away completely, but it
did lose some of its luminescence. "He asked how you two
had been doing, and I thought—"

"Well, there's your answer," Big Joe said, cutting him
off. We didn't need to hear another word.

Kozy spent the next ten minutes showering us with apologies, chatted with Mo for a while after that, then left. Joe
got tired of watching TV and walked over to see Gerald
Gibbons and his thirty-four-foot Airstream Limited. Mo

and I stayed behind and played cards, setting up a table and two lawn chairs just outside Lucille's door. Time went by like molasses running up a steep hill.

Murphy finally called us around three p.m. I sent Mo to get her father while I went to the phone.

"Have you heard about Eddie?" I immediately asked the Capitol Police officer upon picking up the receiver.

"I heard. It's all over the news."

"And?"

"And what? He hasn't been found yet, if that's what you're asking."

"Oh Lord . . ."

"You get the diary back yet?"

"No. Not yet. We expect to have it around five or so." Right after I talked to Eileen, I'd called Dee to confirm that the book was on its way and she'd said that was the estimated time of arrival Federal Express had given her: five p.m. Eastern Time.

"Jesus," Murphy complained. "Why's it taking so long?"

"Never mind that. What did you find out about Carol Dunne?"

"Nothing I can talk about over the phone."

"Does that mean you're coming here to tell us?"

"I'm afraid that's not possible either. Maybe sometime tonight—"

"Sometime tonight? No, sir. No. That's not good enough."

"Excuse me?"

"We had a deal, Officer Murphy, and we've lived up to our end of it. Now it's your turn."

"Mrs. Loudermilk—"

"I don't want to hear any arguments. You told us if we stayed put here at the park, you'd keep us informed of your progress. Every step of the way. Well, we've stayed put, and now we want to know what you've found out. Right this minute. Otherwise . . .''

"Don't say it, Mrs. Loudermilk. I believe you're about to threaten me, and I don't much care for threats."

"I'm not threatening you, Officer Murphy. I'm just telling you, we're not going to sit here on our hands if you're not going to make it worth our while. Especially now that Eddie needs our help more than ever."

He wanted to believe I was bluffing, but he was too smart for that. A mother fearful for her child's safety does not bluff; she just tells you what she intends to do about it, and leaves it at that.

"Okay," Murphy said, sounding worn out. "Okay." He paused a moment, no doubt to curse under his breath. "Your friend Taz's real name is Nelson Charles Plaschke. Alias Taz. Or alias Vlade, depending on the arrest report you're reading. And there's quite a few to choose from, let me tell you. B and E, possession, possession with intent, aggravated assault . . . and forgery."

"Forgery?"

"Yes, ma'am. He's a man of many talents, Mr. Plaschke, but that's apparently his true calling. Forgery. Wills, notes of transfer, rights of attorney, that sort of thing. And of course, checks. Big checks, small checks, personal, pay-roll—you name it, he's written it. He even wrote a few of Carol Dunne's once.

"She had her purse snatched out at Georgetown Park a few years back, and Plaschke ended up with her checkbook. By the time he was picked up, he and a girlfriend had forged her signature on over twenty checks and passed every one of 'em."

"Then he and Dunne *do* know each other."

"At least indirectly, yes."

"But why—"

"I can't tell you the why of it yet, Mrs. Loudermilk. But I think I'll be able to soon. I'll call you again later tonight, huh?"

"But—"

I was talking to a dead phone.

Mo and Big Joe, both of whom had been standing beside me now for some time, looked at me expectantly. "Well? What did he say?" Big Joe asked.

I told them.

"And that's it? That's all he said?" Mo asked when I was finished.

I told her yes, that was all he'd said. We'd sent him off with a hundred questions, and he'd come back with one answer.

Lucky for us he was working for free.

There was a pair of plainclothes detectives watching the trailer park. They were sitting in an unmarked Chevy sedan at the far edge of the parking lot, pretending to be two average citizens who'd been glued to the front seat of their motionless car, helpless to move. They could have just as well come in full uniform, driving a fully badged patrol car with a telescope mounted to the hood. You couldn't have missed them in the dark, let alone in the broad daylight of four o'clock in the afternoon.

I'd been in the process of walking aimlessly through the park when I noticed them, too exhausted to jog, too restless to sit still. Between worrying about Eddie and counting the seconds before five o'clock, when the Wildman diary was scheduled to be returned to us, I was closing fast on a nervous breakdown. When I'd spotted the cops, I was a hair's breadth away from the loudest, most ear-piercing

scream any fifty-four-year-old woman could possibly un-
leash . . .

And then I got called to the phone.

"Who is it?" I asked Mr. Berger, the trailer park manager, who had once more left his office to answer the ringing pay phone outside it when no one else would.

"They didn't say," Berger told me. He shrugged and
smiled, the way gas station attendants used to as they did
your windows and checked your oil. Just happy to be of
service.

I didn't know whether to run *to* the phone, or *away* from
it. If it was news about Eddie, what would it be? That he
had been found by the police, safe and unharmed, and taken
into custody without incident? Or that his body was lying
on a slab somewhere, waiting for me or Joe to identify it?

I picked up the dangling receiver and said, "Hello."

"This Mrs. Loudermilk?"

The voice was familiar, but I couldn't place it.

"That's right. Who is this?"

"This is the man who's got your baby boy, that's who
it is. Just like you've got somethin' of mine."

My heart stopped in midbeat.

"Taz?"

"You remember me. Good."

"What do you mean, you've got my boy?"

"Should I have been more specific? I'm talkin' about
Eddie, Mrs. Loudermilk. Your son. He's here with me—
waiting to die."

I put my hand out to brace myself against the wall of
the manager's building, suddenly feeling very faint.

"How did you get this number?" I asked.

"Girl who answered Angus's phone gave it to me. I figured somebody over there'd have it."

"I don't believe you," I said.

"I'm sorry to hear that. I'll tell Eddie you said good-bye."

"If he's there, let me talk to him!"

"I'd like to do that, Mrs. Loudermilk, but I'm afraid he's in no condition. Besides, we're getting off the subject. And the subject is my book, and how and when you're gonna give it back to me."

"If you're about to suggest we meet you at another crack house somewhere, you can forget it," I said, trying to keep a cool head.

"You'll meet me where I tell you to meet me and like it," Taz said angrily.

"No. We won't. You almost killed us that way once, getting us to come to you. This time, it's going to be different. Otherwise, no deal."

"In that case, Eddie's dead."

I swallowed hard and said, "Then he's dead. And your book is the headline story in all the papers tomorrow." I let that sink in a minute before going on. "You want us to meet with you, it's got to be someplace public. Very public."

"Like where?"

I tried to think of the most crowded and open place I knew of. "Like in the Mall," I said.

"The Mall?"

"That's right. At the Lincoln Memorial. Up at the top of the steps, near the statue."

Taz fell silent, but you could almost hear hot steam escaping from his ears as he considered my proposal. Finally, he said, "Be there in a half hour. With my book."

"I need more time than that," I said. "Make it an hour."

"You've got thirty minutes, Mrs. Loudermilk. I've made all the concessions I'm gonna make today. I don't see you at the Lincoln Memorial in thirty minutes with my book, you better start thinkin' about how you want Eddie dressed for his funeral.''

He hung up.

I did the same and took off running for Lucille.

───── **15** ──

The Lincoln Memorial on a late Saturday afternoon looked like an ant-infested honey jar. It was crawling with people, just as I'd hoped. The Mall before it was no less crowded, despite the fact that D.C.'s weather was changing, segueing rapidly from warm and sunny to overcast and humid. The sudden shift almost appeared to have turned the water in the Mall's two reflecting pools black.

Joe and I had arrived at the Memorial with less than five minutes to spare. My husband's newest friend for life, Gerald Gibbons, had smuggled us out of the trailer park in the back seat of his Ford Bronco and delivered us to the Mall, no questions asked. We were hunched down on the Bronco's floor like so many grocery bags, hoping the two cops I'd spotted in the parking lot earlier wouldn't see us and decide to tag along.

They didn't.

Had we waited for the Wildman diary to be delivered to

the trailer park before making our escape, we would have never made it to the Memorial in time, so we'd been forced to improvise. We found a book in our ever-expanding traveling library about the same size and shape as the diary, wrapped it up in newspaper, then left Mo behind to await the real thing. We told her to ditch the cops watching the park and bring the diary to us at the Memorial as soon as it arrived, just in case Taz saw through our ruse before we could win Eddie's release. If, in fact, Eddie needed releasing.

That Taz was lying about holding our son hostage was a very real possibility, of course. How could he have found Eddie in the first place? we wondered. And yet, it wasn't too hard to answer such questions ourselves, with or without Taz's help. After all, Eddie certainly hadn't broken out of jail just to come running straight to Mommy and Daddy; he would have had a more constructive purpose than that in mind. Like finding Vlade before Vlade could point any more guns in his parents' direction, for example. And if he had "found" him the same way *we* had found him—which was to say, like a moth finds a spider . . .

We'd called the pager number Officer Murphy had given us before leaving the park, but he hadn't responded by the time we'd driven off. Again, Mo was left with instructions to tell him what we were doing, and why, if he called in. We were taking the chance that he would botch things up if he burst in on the scene at the Memorial before we could finish scamming Eddie's supposed kidnapper, but it was a chance we felt we had to take. Because we were hoping this meeting with Taz would end not just with a safe and sound Eddie, but with Taz in police custody as well, and we were realistic enough to know taking Taz in under citizen's arrest was going to be out of the question. He wasn't that tame, and we weren't that tough.

Joe tried to talk me into staying back and out of sight, but in the end, we climbed the Memorial's steps together. It was an arduous climb, and a circuitous one, as we had to weave our way around people taking photographs of one another with nearly every step. In the open foyer above, Abraham Lincoln sat in dignified silence, looking out upon a sea of admirers and the crowded Mall below. Electronic flashes winked and video cameras whirred, as children stood before the giant statue's base and read aloud the words inscribed above Lincoln's head: "In this temple, as in the hearts of the people for whom he saved the Union . . ." Any other time, I might have found the scene very moving, but on this day, all I could think about was Eddie.

Joe and I positioned ourselves at the top of the steps, from where we could look down on the Mall and see anyone approaching from that direction. We were there less than fifteen seconds when someone behind me said, "You like to cut things close, don't you, folks?"

We spun around to find Taz standing there. He must have been up there all the time, off in the back behind the crowd where he couldn't easily be seen.

"That my book?" he asked, eyeing the *Washington Post*–wrapped parcel in my hands.

"Where's our son?" Joe asked him, ignoring his question. Whether it was obvious to Taz or not, it was all Joe could do to keep from reaching for the man's throat and strangling the life out of him.

"Don't worry about Eddie. He's fine."

"I didn't ask how he's doing. I asked where he is."

"Where he is is in a house somewhere. Where all the windows are closed and the gas is turned on. His head isn't in the oven, or anything, but you get the general idea. Somebody doesn't pull him out of there quick . . ." He completed the sentence with a facetious shrug.

"Why, you sonofa—"

Joe leaned forward to go after him, but I was already there to put a hand on his chest. "No, Joe! Don't! You can't!"

"That's right, Joe. You can't," Taz said. He allowed himself a smile before looking over both shoulders to make sure no one had noticed the ugly turn our conversation had taken. "I get the book, you get the address. And if you get there in time, it's a happy ending for everybody. If not . . . it'll probably be because you fucked around too long out here with me. Talking."

Which was his way of asking for the book. Now.

Had the book in my hands been the one he actually wanted, I would have turned it over gladly. But beneath all the newspaper, all I had to offer him was a well-worn copy of something called *The Dynamics of English*, by an author whose name I couldn't even recall. If I gave him the book now, and he opened it here, before telling us where Eddie was, we were doomed. So I had to try to stall him just long enough for Mo to get here with the real Wildman diary, praying all the while that the wait wouldn't kill my son.

"We have some questions first," I said.

"I don't think you understood me, Mrs. Loudermilk," Taz said.

"Eddie's running out of time, yes, I know. But finding him alive isn't going to do him much good if people still think he murdered Emmitt."

"That's not my problem."

"No, it's ours. And I'm telling you, you'll get this book when you answer a couple of questions for us. Not until."

He couldn't believe it. He looked at me, then at Joe, then back at me again. We were a unified front.

"You're crazy," he said, almost laughing.

"This diary is a fake, isn't it?" I asked, referring to the book in my hand as if it were the one he was expecting.

"Who told you that?"

"Carol Dunne. Who else?"

"Carol Dunne? Who's that?"

"The woman who hired you to write this. That's who."

"I don't know what you're talking about," Taz said.

I was glancing away every minute or so to look for Mo, but there was still no sign of her. "You're a forger, Mr. Plaschke. That's what you do. And Carol Dunne hired you to forge one of her boss's diaries. Didn't she?"

"How the hell do you know my name?"

"We know all of your names. Taz; Vlade; Nelson. What we don't know is why someone like Carol Dunne would hire someone like you to fake a U.S. senator's personal diary. Or how your doing so came to get Emmitt Bell murdered."

"What got Emmitt murdered is simple: stupidity," Taz said, sneering. "One, for thinking he could rip me off and get away with it. And two, for ripping off the wr—" He stopped himself abruptly, realizing he was about to say more than he intended.

"The wrong what? The wrong *book*?" I asked excitedly. "Is that what you were going to say?"

"Never mind what I was going to say. The quiz show's over. Either give me the book, or kiss Eddie's ass good-bye." He was still glancing about nervously, fearful of being ambushed.

"Where's our son?" Joe asked him again.

"Right where I kicked his ass and left 'im. The book, Mrs. Loudermilk!" He reached his hand out for it, fresh out of patience.

I looked out over the Mall, but there was still no sign of Mo.

"You, kick Eddie's ass?" Joe asked incredulously.

"That's right. We mixed it up, and he got his ass kicked. Same as you are, you don't—"

Before I knew what was happening, Joe sprang like a cat past me to grab Taz by the throat.

"Joe!"

"He's lyin', Dottie! He hasn't got Eddie!"

Taz was struggling mightily to break Joe's grip, but he wasn't having much success. The three of us hadn't created a scene yet, but we had caused a few heads to turn.

"Joe, we don't know that!" I cried, trying not to shout.

"Look at his face, baby," Joe said, pointing with his free hand at his captive's reddening face. "There ain't a scratch on it!"

Now I saw Joe's point. Our wildcat son has lost a few fights in his life, it's true, but his opponents have always had one thing in common, victorious or otherwise: They looked like they'd been in a fight. With a motorcycle gang. If Taz *had* "mixed it up" with Eddie, he might have emerged from their altercation on top—but not unblemished. And as far as Joe or I could see, there wasn't a mark on him.

"You messed up, boy," Joe said, a self-satisfied grin forming on his face.

That was all Taz needed to hear. Spurred on by Joe's little dig, he at last found the strength to break Joe's grip and shove him aside. Surprised, my husband stumbled backward and fell on his behind, nearly tripping a group of people standing there. I was watching him struggle back to his feet when Taz lurched forward to snatch the book from my hands. He was running down the Memorial's steps before I even knew what hit me.

"Joe! He's getting away!" I screamed, without really thinking.

On his feet again, Big Joe took off after him. What else would he do? He'd interpreted my cry as an order to take up pursuit. But just as he got started—

"Hold on there a minute!"

Finally, all the excitement had attracted the attention of one of the security guards on duty here. He had been standing back near the statue of Lincoln itself, no doubt watching to see that no crazy tried to scale it, but he was moving toward Joe at a fairly crisp pace. Taz wasn't out of sight yet, but he would be soon, and if Joe was detained for more than three seconds by the guard . . .

We couldn't let Taz get away. Not again. He was the key to everything.

So I created a distraction, hoping to draw the guard's attention from Big Joe to me. Don't ask me where I got the idea to do this, because I still haven't figured that out, but I started screaming that I'd seen Lincoln's eyes move.

"I saw his eyes move! He looked right at me! I saw his eyes move!" I cried, running around like someone with hot coals beneath her feet, pointing with both hands like a madwoman.

This is where we came in, remember?

Anyway, my ploy worked. Sort of. I created a scene no one could ignore, including the guard who'd been moving in on Joe. With all eyes focused on me, my husband was free to continue the chase after the soon-to-be-departed Taz . . . only he never did. For some inexplicable reason, he just stood there instead, and endured the humiliation of watching his wife make a complete and total fool of herself. For nothing.

I could have killed him.

It wasn't until the police who'd arrived on the scene had deposited me, in handcuffs, in the back seat of their patrol car that I understood Joe's odd reaction, or lack of same.

There on the Mall, not twenty yards from the base of the Memorial, lay Taz, facedown on the ground, being fitted for his own pair of handcuffs by a man with a familiar face: Bud Early. Dobbs stood nearby, watching him work. Apparently, this was as far as Taz had gotten before running into them, as Joe must have no doubt witnessed.

Too late to save me from becoming a public spectacle, unfortunately.

But I couldn't complain. Taz was in custody, and Eddie, it seemed, was safe.

I sat back and enjoyed my free ride in a police car.

____ 16 __

We ended up downtown again. Sitting in the same drab interrogation room, looking at the same distressed faces, drinking the same stale Metropolitan Police Department coffee. Why we didn't take pictures, I don't know; of everything we'd managed to see of Washington, D.C., over the last six days, I knew we'd remember this place the longest. Why not have some photographs to show the grandchildren?

The good news was, this time around we weren't here to get grilled. Not really. While Harris Murphy was reportedly out hunting down Carol Dunne, armed with the Wildman diary that had finally been returned to us at the trailer park, Mo, Big Joe, and I were here to help Dobbs and Early make some kind of sense out of Taz's official statement, once they were finally able to pry one out of him.

It only took four hours.

And it was a long four hours, too, considering the fact that we still didn't know for sure whether or not Taz's story about Eddie being in some house somewhere with the gas turned on was a lie. We remained confident that it was, yes, but we weren't certain.

So when the two detectives finally made their appearance in our interrogation room, it was hard to say who looked more worn out: them, or us. Early looked like he hadn't shaved in a month, and Dobbs had the lifeless hair of a Lhasa Apso.

The door wasn't closed behind them before I asked them about Eddie.

"Relax. Wherever Eddie is, Mr. Plaschke hasn't seen him," Early said. His usual state of disgruntlement seemed to be something much uglier today.

"Thank God," I said.

Early's only response to that was a cold stare. Then he said, "You need to be put away for life. All three of you."

"You didn't do a damn thing we told you," Dobbs chimed in. "Not a damn thing."

"I'd heard older people have a problem with authority, but you two . . ." Early shook his head to indicate that Joe and I took the cake.

"Jeez Looweez," Big Joe said, not quite far enough under his breath.

Early glared at him from the left, Dobbs from the right. "Excuse me?" Dobbs said.

"My husband said we understand your disappointment, and we apologize," I said, as softly and contritely as I could. "We should have taken your advice and stayed out of this whole mess, but we didn't. It was an error in judgment on our part for which we are all deeply sorry. Really."

"It's a little late for apologies, Mrs. Loudermilk. Don't you think?" Early asked.

"I thought an apology was what you wanted."

"You thought wrong," Dobbs said angrily.

"You don't understand how this town works," Early said. "How little it takes to set things in motion that nobody can stop, once they get moving. People like Carol Dunne . . . When they take a fall, it's always a hard one. For a lot of people. This diary thing you've uncovered is going to set heads rolling around here from now until the year 2000. You watch."

"And we're to blame for that, is that it?" Mo asked.

"To blame for it? No," Dobbs told her. "You're a part of it, that's all. An integral part. And that means you've made enemies you didn't need. Enemies nobody needs, to be perfectly honest with you. That's what Bud and I have been trying to tell you. It's not going to end here for you people. This is something you're going to have to take with you long after your stay in our fair city is over and done with."

"Okay. So we've screwed ourselves," Big Joe said, unable to remain silent any longer. "We appreciate your pointing that out to us. We'll be more careful in Boston, I promise. *Now* will you tell us what the man had to say in there? *Please*?"

Dobbs and Early glanced at each other, as if they were deciding the issue right there on the spot. Anything to maintain our level of discomfort and uncertainty as long as possible.

"He said a lot of things in there," Dobbs said, taking a seat. "Where would you like us to start?"

Mo asked the obvious first question for all of us: "Did he confess to murdering Emmitt?"

"No." Dobbs shook her head.

"Did he tell you who did, at least?" I asked.

"No. He didn't tell us that, either. He says he doesn't know."

That was what he had told Joe and me at the crack house too, but we'd been hoping he might change his story for the police.

"Cheer up," Early said when we all became quiet, our feeble hopes that this might be the end of Eddie's ordeal clearly dashed. "It could've been worse. He could have told us it was Eddie."

He was right, but that wasn't much comfort.

"How did you find us at the Memorial in the first place?" I asked, while the question was still fresh in my mind. I'd been wondering about it ever since my forced removal from the Mall.

"We followed you there, naturally," Dobbs said.

"From the trailer park?"

"In the back of your friend's Ford Bronco, yeah."

"But—"

"You didn't think we'd put just two guys on you, did you? After all the resourcefulness you'd shown us in the past? I don't think so." She shook her head at the absurdity of the thought.

"The boys in the parking lot were decoys, Mrs. Loudermilk," Early said, doing a poor job of repressing a smile. "Detective Dobbs and I were parked about two rows over from your trailer, near something called an Apache Trailblazer. Ever seen one? They're small, but nice. Full kitchen and everything. We borrowed it from one of the guys in Traffic."

Joe looked over at me as if to ask, *Do you feel as stupid as I do at this moment?*

"Score one for the professionals," Dobbs said smugly.

Then the conversation turned back to Taz.

Like Angus had when Murphy questioned him at his town house the night before, Taz had played dumb to start. He hadn't forged anything, he hadn't threatened anybody, and he certainly hadn't killed anybody. Who was Carol Dunne? Who was Ahmed Lee? Who was Emmitt Bell? He'd never heard of any of these people. It wasn't until Dobbs and Early made it clear to him that they had him perfectly fitted for Ahmed's murder that his story began to change. Apparently, he'd left his fingerprints all over the dead man's apartment, and an eyewitness had even placed him on the scene at the time the murder had taken place. You wouldn't think the cops' old "Cooperate, and we might go easy on you" line would still work on anybody, but it does. At least, it did on Taz, once he did away with all the weak denials and tried to sell Dobbs and Early on the idea that he had killed his friend Ahmed only after Ahmed had tried to kill *him* with a baseball bat during an argument over money. Small wonder he and his lawyer decided they'd better play ball with the detectives if they ever wanted such a sorry defense to fly.

The tale Taz inevitably came to tell, once he'd finally started saying something worth hearing, was surprising in some ways, yet predictable in others.

For the most part, it agreed with much of what we already suspected had happened, tenuous as those suspicions were. Just as we thought, Carol Dunne had indeed hired him to forge a Wildman diary. But apparently not for the purpose of blackmailing Senator Dick Meany.

That had been Emmitt's idea, Taz said.

The fake diary Dunne had hired Taz to write was meant to differ from the original she'd supplied him with in only one, relatively harmless way: it omitted several entries embarrassing to Dunne. Specifically, entries that referred to a pair of sexual liaisons she had once had with her employer,

Senator Wildman. No doubt terrified that Wildman might eventually lose his fight to keep his private diaries private, his very married chief of public relations had taken it upon herself to edit the offensive volume, presumably because Wildman himself would not. As near as Taz could remember, Dunne had never mentioned Dick Meany's name, and neither had it appeared so much as once in either copy of the diary.

Meany had only entered the picture when Emmitt did.

Emmitt and Taz hadn't seen each other in months, but one day he'd shown up at Taz's door bearing gifts—some beer and a little coke—acting like they were brothers who'd been separated at birth. Taz had thought nothing of the timing of his visit at the time—Taz had received the original Wildman diary from Dunne only two days before— but now, of course, he could see that it had been anything but coincidence.

In any case, the two drank the beer, did the coke, and talked about old times. And new ones. Emmitt claimed to have seen Taz with Dunne at the Dirksen Building one day, and wondered what was up. It was a question a sober Taz might not have answered, but a loaded one, it seemed, found it a great little conversation starter. Taz told Emmitt everything, happy to have someone he could brag to about the biggest forgery job in his life.

Emmitt had little to say after hearing the story, leaving Taz to think afterward that maybe it hadn't really registered with him. He'd been just as wasted as Taz had been, after all. But three days later, Emmitt came by Taz's place again, this time with a proposition: a thousand dollars for a few extra lines in the forged Wildman diary. Lines which would insert Dick Meany into some of Graham Wildman's most outrageous and politically devastating memoirs.

What the hell, Taz said, why not? As long as he made

the changes Dunne wanted, why should she care if he did the same for someone else?

Taz went on to insert Emmitt's lines, but he never got his money. When it came time to pay up, Emmitt changed the deal. All of a sudden, he decided his thousand dollars should buy him more than the alterations he'd asked for; it should buy him the fake diary itself.

Taz told Emmitt he was crazy.

It wasn't clear to him just how crazy Emmitt was, however, until Emmitt broke into his apartment and stole the forged diary Taz wouldn't sell him. Or what he *thought* was the forged one, anyway. He'd torn Taz's place apart and run off with the first Wildman diary he came across. Unfortunately, the first one he came across, Taz said, was the genuine article. He'd stolen the *real* Wildman diary, the one Dunne had given Taz to forge his copy from.

Needless to say, Taz was now in hot water with Dunne. He had to get the diary back from Emmitt, and fast.

But Emmitt was making himself scarce. Taz couldn't track him down. Only when he resorted to following Emmitt's friends around did he finally catch up to Emmitt again, at the Zoo Room the night Emmitt died. Our son Eddie had led Taz right to him.

But Taz hadn't murdered him. On that point he was adamant.

"Then who the hell did?" Big Joe asked Early, after his and Dobbs's recap of Taz's statement was finished. Dobbs had been called off to the phone several minutes before, so the question was left for Early to field alone.

"You don't really want me to answer that, do you, Mr. Loudermilk?"

I'd been afraid he was going to say something along those lines.

"You mean to tell me you still think Eddie did it?" Joe asked him.

"Yes, sir, I do. Granted, we know a great deal more about what Bell was doing there that night than we did before, but . . . as far as the actual circumstances of his death are concerned . . . nothing's really changed, has it? Eddie's still the one who had the fight with him, Eddie's still the one who was doing his girlfriend, and it's still Eddie's knife he was killed with. None of the rest really matters."

"You're nuts," Joe said.

"Really," I agreed.

Early was about to defend himself when the door opened and Dobbs stepped through it to rejoin us. To Early, she said, "That was their friend Murphy. It looks like Ms. Dunne has decided to make a confession of her own."

Wonderful, I thought. *Everybody's making confessions, but nobody wants to admit to having killed Emmitt Bell.*

Maybe Eddie had been smart to break out of jail after all.

"Come on, Mom. He'll be okay," Mo said.

We were eating a wonderful dinner in a charming little café called Afterwords in Dupont Circle, which sat at the back of a bookstore filled with artsy types and college students, all looking very chic and brainy. The food was excellent and the atmosphere was nice, but, as my daughter had noticed, I didn't have much use for either. I was too busy being worried sick about Eddie.

Five days of busting our tails trying to extricate him from the mess he was in, and all we'd really managed to do was expose an American political scandal that was already fast becoming a news story of Watergate-like proportions. Not only was Eddie still on the hook for Emmitt Bell's murder, but he was now a fugitive from justice, something he might not have become had his meddlesome parents not given him reason to believe they were bound and determined to kill themselves trying to clear his name. Instead of improving the boy's situation, we'd just made it worse.

So enjoying a good meal less than two hours after Dobbs and Early had granted us our freedom was a little bit beyond me, as it was for Mo and Big Joe. However, I was the only one at our table acting like a manic-depressive on holiday.

"He didn't kill that boy," I said, to anyone who cared to listen, be they members of the family or total strangers. "He didn't."

"We know that, baby," Joe said, throwing one of his huge arms around me.

"If it was Taz, there has to be a way we can prove it. There *has* to be."

"Mom . . ." Mo started to say.

"We missed something. We must have. Something somebody said or did . . ."

My husband and daughter just looked at me, resigned to the fact that I was going to go on like this no matter what they said to quiet me. I let them look.

"We're going to go back over everything. From the very beginning," I said. "Starting right now."

I sat back and waited for one or both of them to complain, but neither did. All Joe did was push his plate away and say, "Okay. Let's do it."

We didn't leave out a thing. We started with our arrival at Angus's town house Monday night, and finished with our just concluded meeting with Dobbs and Early downtown, and there wasn't a detail left unmentioned in between, no matter how small or innocuous. If we could remember it, we discussed it, and discussed it again. And again.

And it changed absolutely nothing.

No matter how we looked at it, from what angle or from whose perspective, it always added up to the same thing: a puzzle with a hole punched out of it. And at the center of that hole was a man with three names: Nelson Plaschke, a.k.a. Taz/Vlade. Depending on where we were in our review, sometimes he was Taz, and sometimes he was Vlade. Vlade was Eddie's friend from the basketball courts; Taz was the man Stacy had once answered the door for. Taz was the forger Carol Dunne had hired, and Vlade was the friend Emmitt had taken calls from at Curtis Howell's apartment. Taz—

"Wait a minute," Big Joe said at one point, suddenly looking inspired.

Mo wouldn't ask, so I did. "What?"

"Something doesn't jibe here."

"What? What doesn't jibe?"

"Curtis Howell said Emmitt always called Taz 'Vlade' when he talked to him over the phone, right? Not 'Taz' but 'Vlade'—isn't that what he said?"

I had to think about it for a moment before answering. "That's right. He said Emmitt kept dropping the name Vlade. So?"

"So it should be safe to assume that that was the name Emmitt generally used for him, shouldn't it? Vlade, and not Taz?"

"Yes, Daddy, yes," Mo said, exasperated. "So what's your point?"

"My point is, if Emmitt knew Taz as 'Vlade,' and it was Emmitt who introduced him to Angus—"

"Shouldn't Angus have known him as 'Vlade,' as

well?'' I said, picking up on my husband's vibe, albeit somewhat belatedly.

"Yes. Shouldn't he have? Yet he acted like he'd never heard the name before when we asked him about it three days ago. In fact, he only admitted knowing the man at all after Stacy told us about Taz's visit to his home that day. Why? Why wouldn't he tell us he knew the man, unless . . .''

"Unless he was trying to hide something,'' I said.

"Or protect somebody,'' Mo added thoughtfully.

"Like himself, maybe?'' Joe asked.

Without saying another word, we paid our check and left.

"I'm sorry, Mrs. Loudermilk, but I'm really very busy right now,'' Angus said.

He had his front door open just a crack, leading one to believe he had little intention of inviting me in.

"Please, Angus. I have to talk to you. It's an emergency,'' I said, tears welling up in my eyes. I was out there on the porch all alone, and I was shivering against the night cold like an orphan left out on the street.

"This can't wait until morning?'' Angus asked.

"No! I have to talk to you now! Otherwise . . .'' I let my voice trail off and shook my head, as if the rest of the thought were too terrible to contemplate.

He made me wait another full minute, then let me in.

"I can only give you a couple of minutes,'' he said, not so much leading me into the living room as going there himself and assuming I would follow. He looked like he was ready for bed.

We sat down opposite each other and waited, he for me and I for him. He broke before I did.

"Well? What's so important?''

I gave him another minute to appreciate my grieved expression, then said, "You have to tell the truth, Angus. Please."

He seemed genuinely perplexed. "What?"

"Eddie will kill you if you don't. He means it. Please don't let it come to that. Please."

I wiped a single tear from my left cheek with a forearm.

"What the hell are you talking about?" Angus demanded, getting a little edgy.

"I'm talking about Emmitt," I said. "Eddie knows, Angus. He knows it was you who killed him."

"What?"

"You have to give yourself up. You have to go to the police right now and tell them everything. Otherwise, Eddie's going to find you, and . . . and . . ." I choked on the end of the sentence, then went on. "I begged him to let me come here and talk to you first. Before he did anything crazy. He said if I could convince you to turn yourself in, he'd leave you alone. He gave me his word!"

I wasn't hysterical, exactly, but I could have passed for it.

Meanwhile, Angus was losing it. Again. Just as he had when Murphy put the screws to him.

"You've seen Eddie?" he asked me, having suddenly forgotten to be belligerent.

"He says it was *your* idea to have Taz put Dick Meany's name in that diary, not Emmitt's," I said, pretending not to have heard his question. "Emmitt wasn't that creative, he said."

"Where? Where's Eddie now, Mrs. Loudermilk?"

"He says you killed him because he tried to extort money from Meany, instead of just demanding that Meany take his bill off the floor, or something. It was hard to understand a lot of what he said, he was so *furious*—"

"That's a lie! I didn't—"

"I've tried to tell him it's not his place to judge you, but he won't listen! And if you don't turn yourself in to the authorities by tomorrow morning—"

I was cut off by a sudden, urgent knock on the door.

"Oh, my God," I said. "Oh, sweet Jesus . . ."

Angus was as white as a sheet.

"Please, Angus. Please," I pleaded with him. "You have to go, before it's too late!"

"Dottie! Come on out of there, woman!"

Big Joe pounded on the front door again.

"Baby, no!" I shouted back. "I know what I'm doing!"

Angus said nothing, from all appearances unable to move or speak.

"The hell you do!" Joe said, suddenly in the room with us. I'd taken the opportunity to leave the door open for him when Angus had allowed me to trail him into the living room.

"Joe, I have to *try* . . ." I said.

"You wanna be here when the boy gets here? Do you? So they can force you to testify against him later?"

"No, but—"

"He's crazy, Dottie. I told you that. We can't save this man. Nobody can. Now come on and let's get out of here, before it's too late!" He grabbed my hand and started pulling me out of the room, back the way he had come in.

"No! No!" I cried, fighting him off with all my might.

"He'll kill us, too, he finds us in here with him! Don't you understand that?"

"Wait a minute!" Angus snapped, no longer able to endure the bizarre scene he was witnessing in silence. "You have to tell him—"

"We can't tell that boy anything!" Joe barked back at him, holding one of my wrists in each of his giant hands so that I could no longer beat upon his chest unmercifully.

"And we're all through tryin'! You can do what you want—just sit on your ass and wait for him here, if that'll make you happy. I don't really give a damn. But *we're* gettin' the hell out of his way!"

"Joe! Please!" I begged.

But he didn't say another word, preferring instead to guide me toward the front door, still kicking and scratching like a cat being dragged by its tail. Stacy and Eileen appeared from the back of the house just in time to see us go out. They had the horrified look on their faces of two people who'd just stumbled onto a train wreck in the middle of their own backyard.

Joe and I continued our noisy show of marital discord until we were halfway around the block, then sprinted the rest of the way to our truck, laughing like a pair of kids on a great first date.

"Well?" Mo asked us when we'd joined her in the truck's cab. "What do you think?"

I looked past her at Joe, still grinning and out of breath, and said, "I think that was a lot of fun, whether it works or not."

Joe just nodded his head; then we both fell out laughing all over again.

___ 17 __

Angus never did turn himself in.

At least, not technically speaking. He ended up confessing to Emmitt Bell's murder, all right, but he didn't leave his home to do it. Dobbs and Early dropped in on him early Sunday morning, as fate would have it, and found him in a surprisingly talkative mood.

Surprising to most people, anyway.

Not unlike his friend Taz, Angus was copping a self-defense plea too. According to his version of events, he'd heard Eddie and Stacy arguing that Monday night about who should or should not go to meet Emmitt at the Zoo Room following Emmitt's phone call to the house, and when Eddie won the honors and left, Angus had been right behind him. As Joe and I had surmised, Emmitt had turned his blackmail plot against Dick Meany completely upside down, turning what was supposed to be a political act into a strictly criminal one, and Angus was going to try one last time to stop him before his big mouth and wounded pride could ruin them both.

He'd waited outside the Zoo Room until Eddie had his say with Emmitt and left, not wanting our son to see him. When in his haste to get away Eddie dropped his knife on the sidewalk outside the club, Angus, hidden in the shadows of the alley nearby, had seen it fall. He was picking it up when Emmitt crawled through the Zoo Room's bathroom window and dropped into the alley himself, presumably because he'd been spooked by the sight of Taz inside. An argument ensued. Angus tried to convince Emmitt to revert to their original plan for the forged Wildman diary, while Emmitt basically told him to go to hell. Emmitt got angry, and then he got physical. Allegedly. Angus said he had no choice; it was either use Eddie's knife, or die.

He chose to use Eddie's knife.

I thought it was a fine confession, as far as such things went, yet if you wanted to read about it in the *Washington Post*, you had to turn to page 2, because Carol Dunne had the front page all to herself. Tearful, frank, and utterly repentant as she was, one couldn't help but feel sorry for the poor girl. All she'd really wanted was to protect her happy marriage from Senator Wildman's impropriety, and what she'd earned for all her trouble was the blinding white floodlight of public scrutiny. In a city teeming with dark deeds done for motives much uglier and less substantial than hers, she didn't seem very deserving of all the infamy—until you remembered her hatchet man, Taz.

Suddenly, it wasn't all that difficult to condemn her after all.

By late Sunday afternoon, most people in the nation's capital were satisfied that the mystery of Emmitt Bell's murder had been solved: Eddie's roommates, Stacy and Eileen; Lieutenant Harris Murphy of the U.S. Capitol Police;

even those twin towers of police distrust and skepticism, Detectives Angie Dobbs and Bud Early. All the major holes in the puzzle had been filled; only minor details remained to be determined. The entire affair was finally a picture from which nothing was missing . . .

. . . except for Eddie.

As late as three o'clock that afternoon, he still hadn't turned up. He hadn't been seen or heard from in over two days. He was no longer the subject of a frantic police man-hunt, as recent events had forced the authorities to down-grade his status from suspected murderer to escaped convict, but he was still a wanted man, and it was amazing to me how completely he had managed to disappear. I kept expecting a phone call or a relayed message of some kind saying he was alive and well, but I never did receive one.

To say that I was sick about it would be overstating things, but not by much. I just knew he had to be seriously hurt somewhere, unable to walk or get to a phone . . . Maybe he'd been shot and left for dead. Maybe he hadn't eaten a thing in two days, and was dying of starvation. Maybe—

"Mother, you can't go on like this," Mo finally said to me at one point that Sunday, tired of watching me pace Lucille's floor like an animal in a cage. "You just have to pray and have faith that he's okay, wherever he is."

"I know, I know," I said. "I'm trying, really. It's just that . . . I just can't stop *wondering*—"

Big Joe let out a howl. "All right! Way to jump on it, Hurt! That's the way, baby! Hell, yes!"

He was in the bedroom, watching another baseball game on TV. Shoes off, feet up on the bed, a full can of beer by his side. From what I could make out of the play-by-play from where Mo and I stood, somebody named Thomas had just hit a home run. For the Sox. The man didn't say Red or White, he just said "Sox." I tried to remember if I'd ever heard of a player named Thomas Hurt before, but I couldn't. I figured he must be a rookie.

I went into the bedroom to take a closer look at my husband. To marvel at his ability to reduce all his problems to a simple question of runs scored versus runs scored against. It was beyond belief. A woman's way of handling trouble is to tackle it head-on; a man's is to shoot it to death with the remote control until something good shows up on cable.

"Joe, what are you doing?" I asked my husband as Mo joined us in the room, sensing a certain Dottie Loudermilk tension in the air.

"Huh? I'm watchin' the game, baby," Joe said, never once taking his eyes off the set to address me directly.

"I can see you're watching the game. What I'm asking you is, *how* can you do it?"

"How?" He still hadn't looked up at me.

"Yes, *how*. I want to know. I want to try and understand. How can you sit there and watch that stupid baseball game when your son has been missing for two days? Is the power of sport so overwhelming that you can't even spare a moment to worry about the safety of your own flesh and blood?"

Now he understood that he was in serious trouble. He looked up from the television and said, "Baby . . ."

"Yes?"

He let out a heavy sigh. "It's not that I'm not just as concerned about the boy as you are. Because I am. But . . . this helps me to relax, okay? It helps me *cope*. What's wrong with that?"

"What's wrong with it is that there are times in our lives when we should not be *able* to relax. We should not be able to cope. All we should be able to do is *worry*. Some things are that important, Joe. Eddie is that important.''

"I know that. You think I don't know that?''

"Then what the hell are you doing watching a *baseball game*? At a time like this, how can you possibly care who can hit a baseball the farthest, or score the most runs in nine innings, or—''

"Okay, okay! I confess! I was in here watching sports on TV when I should have been in the bathroom cutting my wrists! Forgive me!'' He grabbed the remote control beside him and turned off the television.

"Daddy, I think you're missing Mom's point,'' Mo said.

"No I'm not. She thinks I'm a sports addict! Somebody with no control over themselves!''

"She didn't say that.''

"Can I help it if I like to watch a game or two on the tube every now and then? It's *baseball*, Dottie, not heroin! Sports is what we men do. If we're not watchin' it, we're playin' it. What's the harm in that?''

"She didn't say there was any harm in it. She just said—''

She stopped when she realized Joe was no longer listening to her. He was looking at me, distracted by the odd expression that I now understand had suddenly come over my face.

"What is it?'' he asked me. "What?''

"Say that again,'' I told him.

"Say what again?''

"What you said about men and sports. Just now.''

"What? Sports is what we men do?''

"No, no, after that. You said something about, 'If we're not watching it . . .' ''

" 'We're playin' it.' Yeah, so?''

I took a moment to answer him, still running something over in my mind.

"I just had a thought,'' I said.

* * *

We got directions from Stacy and drove out to Meridian Hill Park. It wasn't the greenest or friendliest-looking park I'd ever seen, but on a Sunday afternoon in August, it was not totally without some late-summer charm. There were long stretches of flat grass, stands of assorted shade trees, baseball diamonds, a kiddie playground . . . and a basketball court. A crowded basketball court.

Crowded or no, the player we'd come here to find wasn't hard to pick out. He was the only one there who looked like a Loudermilk.

"I don't believe it," Mo said.

I turned to face Joe. "Well? Do you want to go get him, or should I?"

Joe shook his head solemnly and said, "If I go out there, woman, there's gonna be a murder at center court. You go."

So I did. I just walked right on over there, stepped onto the court, and grabbed Eddie by the ear as he was going up for a rebound. He squealed like a stuck pig.

"Ow!"

"You don't know what 'ow' is yet," I told him as I pulled him off the court, using his ear for a leash, "but you're going to find out. Just watch."

"Mom! What the hell—"

"You've got time to come out here to play basketball, but not to call your parents or your friends to let them know you're okay. So they can stop worrying about you for two seconds."

"I was gonna call today! Really!"

"That's a lie. And you can tell it to the police, not me."

"The police? What—"

I told him to shut up and keep moving.

By the time we delivered him to Dobbs and Early early

that evening, we'd heard all of the boy's incredible explanations for his behavior that we cared to. He'd broken out of jail to protect us; he hadn't called us for fear that the phones at the trailer park were being tapped; he'd spent the last two days over at a friend's house.

Yes, a *female* friend.

Why wasn't I surprised?

Mo wanted to strangle him, and Joe very nearly did. They had every right to want him dead, and so did I. He had, after all, however inadvertently, made a shambles of Joe's and my dream visit to the nation's capital, Washington, D.C. We never did enter the White House; take the elevator to the top of the Washington Monument; see all the white headstones at Arlington Cemetery; or tour the F.B.I. Building. Half of what we'd always planned to do here, we'd been unable to do, thanks to Eddie.

But man, did we have *fun*.

If that sounds crazy to you, you either don't have kids of your own—or you don't have any like *ours*.

We got the last five ever made.